# Heavenly HACKED

RECKLESS BASTARDS MC
MAYHEM

WALL STREET JOURNAL & USA TODAY BESTSELLING AUTHOR
## KB WINTERS

# Copyright and Disclaimer

This book is a work of fiction. The names, characters, places and incidents are products of the writer's imagination and have been used fictitiously and are not to be construed as real. Any resemblance to persons, living or dead, actual events, locales or organizations is entirely coincidental.

Copyright © 2018 Book Boyfriends Publishing

All rights reserved. No part of this publication may be reproduced, stored in or introduced into a retrieval system, or transmitted, in any form, or by any means (electronic, mechanical, photocopying, recording, or otherwise) without the prior written permission of the copyright owner. The author acknowledges the trademarked status and trademark owners of various products referenced in this work of fiction, which have been used without permission. The publication/use of the trademarks is not authorized, associated with, or sponsored by the trademark owners.

# Table of Contents

Copyright and Disclaimer ................................. ii

Chapter One ............................................................ 7

Chapter Two ......................................................... 19

Chapter Three ...................................................... 31

Chapter Four ........................................................ 49

Chapter Five ......................................................... 55

Chapter Six ........................................................... 63

Chapter Seven ...................................................... 79

Chapter Eight ....................................................... 93

Chapter Nine ...................................................... 111

Chapter Ten ........................................................ 119

Chapter Eleven ................................................... 135

Chapter Twelve .................................................. 149

Chapter Thirteen ................................................ 157

Chapter Fourteen ............................................... 173

Chapter Fifteen .................................................. 185

Chapter Sixteen .................................................. 191

| | |
|---|---|
| Chapter Seventeen | 203 |
| Chapter Eighteen | 217 |
| Chapter Nineteen | 237 |
| Chapter Twenty | 255 |
| Chapter Twenty-One | 269 |
| Chapter Twenty-Two | 279 |
| Chapter Twenty-Three | 291 |
| Chapter Twenty-Four | 301 |

# Heavenly Hacked

Reckless Bastards MC

By Wall Street Journal & USA Today Bestselling Author

KB Winters

# HEAVENLY HACKED

## Chapter One

*Jag*

Everything had gone to shit tonight. Everything that could go wrong did, starting with the fucking shootout at Bungalow Three. At least none of the girls were seriously injured. A few scrapes and bruises from flying glass and grabby gangsters but no life threatening injuries. Even Stitch, who'd managed to take a bullet, had a through and through that would heal in time. The doctor we kept on the payroll showed up about five minutes before the law did and was taking care of it. Discreetly.

It was bad enough the Killer Aces and their stupid ass leader, Genesis, had come to town thinking they'd leave with Lasso's wife and baby. But at the whorehouse, we'd put down a couple members of Roadkill MC, along with a few Killer Aces. Now wasn't the time but it wouldn't be long before my club, the

Reckless Bastards, had them in our crosshairs. Those fuckers had been playing with us long enough and it was time to make them pay.

"Yo, Jag! Some hottie with blue hair is looking for ya." The words registered but the voice didn't, not with so much shit going on. Cops and forensics had showed up and they were taking their sweet ass time looking around. Luckily Lasso and Rocky were already on their way to the hospital after a brutal run-in with her ex. Because there were so many cars, vans and trucks clogging up the place, nothing bigger than a bike would be able to get through.

It shouldn't be all that hard to find a chick with blue hair. I scanned the cluster of people beyond the crime scene tape until my gaze landed on a halo of bright blue hair. Her skin was pale and appeared deceptively delicate, until I saw the sleeve of tattoos on her left arm, fully on display thanks to a sleeveless Grateful Dead t-shirt. She looked around, her gaze freezing when she finally spotted me.

# HEAVENLY HACKED

I didn't recognize her and as I drew closer I knew I'd never met her before. I would have remembered those unusual gray eyes. "You're looking for me?" I asked, wary of this bundle of contradictions.

She nodded and her smile was soft, almost affectionate like we knew each other. "I am." She seemed stunned to see me, which I found odd considering she'd sought me out.

"Look, this isn't really a good time for you to be here. Who are you really looking for because I don't know you?"

"No," she sighed. "You don't. Not technically." Her shoulders fell but only for a second before she recovered, once again squaring her shoulders and looking at me head on. "But I am looking for you, Jeremiah. It's me, Vivi."

That one word. That name sucked all the air out of my lungs. It was a name I'd like to say I hadn't thought about in the past almost fifteen years, but the truth was, Vivi had crossed my mind on more than a few occasions over the years. "Wow. Vivi. How the hell are you? What are you doing here? How did you find me?"

She let out a long slow breath and raked a hand through her blue hair. "Not bad but I've been better. Do you have a minute?" She looked nervous as hell but good. Healthy. Not strung out. Thank fucking goodness.

I really wished I could stay and chat but too much shit needed to get done and Cross needed my help. "Tonight's not good for me, Vivi. Where you staying at?" I let out a long breath. It was still surreal to say her name and have her here in front of me. I'd spent the better part of my childhood wishing for that very thing.

"It's Vegas," she said simply. "Finding someplace to stay is the easy part. If you get un-busy in the next couple days, give me a call." She handed me a business card, all black with raised silver lettering. *Vivi M.* was all it said. "It was nice to finally meet you in real life, Jeremiah."

Yeah it was. Too damn bad that she hadn't wanted to meet all those years before. But that was water under the bridge. She'd looked me up because she clearly needed something, and when I had a free moment I'd give her a call and see what that was.

"You too. I'll give you a call as soon as I can."

"Yeah, okay." She said as she turned to walk away. She sounded doubtful, but I had things to do and now wasn't a good time.

I needed to check on Lasso and especially Rocky. She'd taken a few nasty hits to the face and her pregnant belly and I knew Lasso had to be out of his fucking mind right now.

My club and my brothers were my first priority.

As much as I hated it, Vivi would have to wait.

***

Seeing Vivi had brought up so many memories and made it hard to sleep. Which was what I really needed after the craziness of the past few months. But instead of closing my eyes and drifting off to sleep, I could see it clear as day. The last good memory I'd ever had.

"I just picked up an extra shift, honey." As soon as I came in from school, Mom was already dressed in her purple scrubs and matching sneakers with hot pink laces. She smiled at me, searching for signs that I was disappointed she was going back to work. Again.

I understood even though I wished she didn't have to work so hard. "You know I could help out with the bills, Mom."

She shook her head as I knew she would, her chin-length bob brushing her jaw. "Absolutely not, kid. Even if I worked every day for the rest of my life I can't afford to send you to any of those schools already sniffing around here. Save the money from your little jobs."

I grinned because it wasn't all that little. In fact, it was enough to get me through two years at a top tier college and maybe the full four at a state school.

## HEAVENLY HACKED

*But she never asked so I didn't tell her. Yet. I planned to let her know the day of my high school graduation. Three years away. "I had to ask even though you're a stubborn ol' mule."*

*"Who you callin' old?" She winked and slipped on the sweater I bought two Christmases ago because she was forever complaining that the hospital was too cold. "There's stuff in the fridge for stir-fry and your lunch tomorrow. Eat your veggies."*

*"Okay, Mom. I hear you."*

*She rolled her eyes and kissed my cheek. "Don't be on that computer all night Jeremiah. Get outside and live a little. Show that beautiful smile to a pretty girl."*

*I rolled my eyes because pretty girls looked right through me, but she wouldn't believe that because she wore mom blinders. Constantly.*

*"Did you pack a meal for yourself, Mom?"*

*"Salad and a sandwich. See you later honey. And don't hack any more government agencies."*

*Her laughter stayed even after she was long gone and my shoulders relaxed. Getting caught hacking the FBI could have ended much differently if not for the excuse of my police officer father's death just two months before they caught me. No one said anything about the forced entries they found prior to his death, much to my great relief. They found I was cheaper than other security experts but it allowed me to sock away a nice college fund.*

*College was a few years away. Right now, all I wanted to do was to talk to NextGen, also known as NextGen_4@5. She was my best friend even though we'd never met in real life. It didn't matter because we talked almost every day, voice or text chat. I preferred voice chat but sometimes she couldn't and she wouldn't say why. I didn't push because I knew all about fucked up home situations. Dad was killed three years ago and Mom had only returned to normal this past year.*

"Calling NextGen." The ringing sound was loud in the kitchen where my laptop sat on the far end of *the counter while I pulled out the ingredients for the stir-fry.*

*"Jeremiah, what's up homie?"*

*I couldn't help but grin at her attempts to be cool. "Vivi, I told you never to say that."*

*"You said you weren't offended."*

*"I'm not but you sound incredibly ... white."*

*She paused for a second and I thought maybe I'd pissed her off, something I thought was impossible. Vivi was a tough girl. A bad ass. Then she burst out laughing. "I am actually super white. The old lady next door says I'm practically see through."*

*"And when you say homie, you sound it. How'd that intrusion code work out?"*

*"Great. It took longer than I would've liked but I got in and looked around, found some interesting data before adding a back door for later."*

*"Untraceable?"*

"Is there any other way?" Unlike the girls at my school, Vivi was confident and she had no problems being sarcastic as hell.

"I seem to remember one key time when you did leave a trace."

"One time! One damn time and you're never gonna let me forget it!" I could hear the laughter in her voice because we both knew I'd never let her forget.

"One time is all it takes. Believe me, I know."

"Fine, smart ass. What are you doing?"

"Making dinner. Mom's workin' a double. You?"

"Just some scout work for an investigator I know who doesn't mind hiring a fourteen year old girl." She was always doing work like that, for guys with no scruples. "Don't worry, I got half the fee up front like you suggested."

"Maybe if we meet up in the real world, I could act as your body guard when you meet these people." Yeah it was a coward's way to ask her about meeting in person but I wasn't ready for that kind of rejection.

## HEAVENLY HACKED

"Maybe," she said but she didn't mean it. "It's not like either of us can travel on our own."

That was bullshit. "Well one of us does plenty on her own that she probably shouldn't."

"Which is why she can't have people asking questions about unaccompanied minors staying overnight. I'm sorry Jeremiah, but not now."

I sighed and nodded even though she couldn't hear me.

I'd ask her to meet three more times over the next two years. Vivi always said no and when my mom caught a bullet from a deranged shooter in the hospital, I stopped trying.

I took the hint and stopped asking.

A few months later, I stopped messaging and calling her altogether.

Hers was the longest friendship of my life and it mattered more to me than I knew. Until it was gone. But she clearly hadn't felt the same so when I walked into that Army recruitment center, I put all my *thoughts of NextGen behind me and moved on with my life.*

*My single, solitary life.*

## Chapter Two

*Vivi*

The sun was high up in the sky and shining bright as I peeked through the blinds of my hotel room. I was high up enough that I didn't need to *peek* but being on edge didn't just go away because I'd checked into a luxury hotel in the flashiest city in the whole damn country. It was still hard to believe that I'd finally set eyes on Jeremiah after all these years.

He wasn't quite how I pictured him. He was bigger and taller than I imagined, even when I added on a decade for age and life. His skin was dark and smooth, like mahogany silk and I bet it was just as soft to the touch. But Jeremiah had more muscles than I imagined a computer geek having. But, then again, I'd never imagined him as a solider or a biker.

I only wished it hadn't taken a shit show of the highest order to finally get me to reach out to him.

But right now the shit show had to take precedence above all else because there was someone—at least *one* someone—who wanted me dead. This wasn't your typical, *I'm gonna kill you* kind of death threat. I was used to those.

As a cyber security expert, and a woman, there was always *that* guy who got pissed when you breached his unbreachable wall or found the hidden, double encrypted folder he thought he was clever enough to hide in a partition. They always got pissed and then assured me that I'd regret it. I wasn't sure what I was supposed to regret.

This though, this was something different that stemmed from a pretty routine job. I worked with people with the most secrets to hide, massive international corporations. I hated them all, but they paid well to make sure no one could get into their secrets and tell the world. And on occasion I took some *fun* work just to keep life interesting. My latest was a routine deep dive for a government agency that shall not be named. They gave me the data to sort, clean and

## HEAVENLY HACKED

back up redundantly before I handed it over in exchange for a big fat ... *bank transfer*. Didn't have the same ring to it as *check* but the zeroes were fat enough for a clean getaway.

Like this one.

I'd been sorting and cleaning when I came upon a few photos that some asset whose name I didn't know had somehow gotten access to and handed over to a handler—whom I knew—but called Bob. And since Bob was a woman, I was pretty sure that was an alias.

Riding from New York to Vegas on my Suzuki V-Strom had given me a lot of time to think about what I'd seen. Given the quality of the break-in that sent me running, it was down to the governor with the underage side piece or the snitching drug lord who met frequently with suits too ugly and cheap to be anything but Feds.

The break-in at my New York apartment was a pro job. Not so good that I didn't detect it but good enough that someone less paranoid than me might miss the telltale signs. But now as I logged into the camera I'd set up when I started taking off-the-books work for the government—my paranoia at work—I wondered if it was as bad as I made it out to be in my head. But as soon as the feed came to life, I knew that I hadn't. Not only was I not prone to overreacting but I prided myself for being levelheaded.

The decoy electronics I'd left behind, including a laptop, digital camera, a handful of flash drives and a virus-ridden external hard drive, were all missing. I eagerly rewound the footage to see who I'd be spying on later. My money was on the governor because I assumed a drug kingpin would just blow up the whole building to be safe. Those guys never worried about innocent bystanders; they dealt in certainty.

*I think.*

Going back twelve hours in the footage, I spotted an unfamiliar face. White male, approximately thirty with a bald head and a hint of a tattoo on one hand. Otherwise, he was unidentifiable.

I captured the image and sent it off to one of my sources. I knew it would be the best way to identify him.

## HEAVENLY HACKED

My source and I were close, but not like *friends*. It didn't matter. People like me didn't need friends, not when I was buried in a task like pulling up remote access on the decoy devices so I could see who had them and maybe even where they were. I'd made extra certain that the person who grabbed the devices would feel safe. The devices hadn't been turned on, but I'd be alerted when they were.

Another task done, and I looked toward the window again, desperate for a few hours in the sunshine. Maybe poolside. But my life didn't stop just because I was in danger. I had a couple of private clients I needed to focus on, especially if this current shit show put my security clearance in danger. It was easy work, just doing a regular sweep of the security footage to make sure none of his employees were stealing. It was a pretty solitary life and transferred just as well to a transient one, which made working on the run a cinch.

But even cynical hermits like me got hungry so I put on some clothes and went in search of food. It was

23

early evening and I still hadn't heard form Jeremiah so it was safe to assume I probably wouldn't. Not that I could blame him. We were strangers to one another after all this time and if he had shown up on my doorstep, I might not have been as welcoming. In fact, I might have been damned hostile if some strange man came knocking asking for a favor. And it looked like Jeremiah and his friends had enough trouble of their own.

\*\*\*

As I dug into my steak burger and herbed fries, I grew frustrated with myself. Sure this would probably go a lot smoother if I could combine Jeremiah's computer skills with my own, but I didn't *need* him. I could do this without him and without getting myself killed, so why in the hell was I waiting around for him?

I paid the check and went back to my room. It was time to fight back and for a girl like me that meant gathering intel. People left all kinds of shit about themselves out in the world, particularly on the

## HEAVENLY HACKED

Internet, especially politicians eager to prove they were as normal as the average Joe.

They rarely were, and I knew Governor Blaise of Florida was far from what his voters might consider *normal*. Bank statements, web browsing history, photo searches and reverse photo searches yielded plenty of information. And that was the easy part.

Cell phone data was even easier, but my favorite source was the credit agencies. They had shitty security and they made it easy to get in, grab what I needed and get the fuck out before anyone even knew I'd been there. It was so easy it made me think of the black hats I knew who pulled in more cash for one job than I sometimes cleared all year. If I was into it, I'd be a very rich woman.

Instead, I was caught up with some bullshit that was bound to get me killed.

\*\*\*

"There's no need to pay it all today, Miss. I'm sure we could get you financing with favorable rates." This guy was my second least favorite guy on the planet, the one who flashed that smarmy smile while trying to convince me he wasn't screwing me over.

"How about I pay cash in full today and you knock a few grand off the top?" He wasn't the only one who could negotiate, but I was much better at it.

"That's not going to happen. My boss won't go for it." Steepled hands and dimpled smile meant to disarm me only put me more on alert.

"Then get him in here and let me explain how this works, *Kyle*." I was annoyed and though it wasn't all his fault, it was enough of his fault that I felt no guilt about taking it all out on him. I'd been in Vegas for two days now and Jeremiah hadn't reached out, which meant I was wrong about him. And I hated being wrong. "Please. Look I want to buy this camper and drive it off the lot today, but your price is too high and there are at least three thousand miles on it already."

## HEAVENLY HACKED

"I'll see what I can do." Kyle left me alone, probably called me a few bitches under his breath while he either wasted time or actually went to get approval from his boss.

It gave me time to think, something I'd been doing a lot lately.

As a kid, Jeremiah would have jumped right into the middle of things to help me out, but this older, buffer, military-biker Jeremiah? A totally different man altogether. And when I woke up that morning, I knew I was on my own. So I'd put my bike in a storage facility and took a bus to Sahara where there were dozens of car dealerships. If this Kyle character couldn't get me a deal, someone else would.

I had plenty of cash and I was ready to go off the grid. At least by all appearances. By the time Kyle returned with the paperwork and the sale was complete—five thousand dollars cheaper—I was tired, hungry and ready to settle in for the night. But I needed provisions so I could stay low-key for a while.

Armed with a brand new to me 2018 Winnebago Spirit camper, I drove to the nearest grocery store and stocked up on pretzels, chips, mustard and diet root beer, snacks I'd eaten since I was a kid. With my router and a parking pass at one of the casinos on the old part of the Strip, I was ready to get to work.

***

I set my laptop on the dinette, opened it up to connect to the encrypted voice chat and grabbed a root beer.

"Hey babe, whatcha got for me?"

I smiled at my friend Peaches and her over the top greeting. "Hey Peaches, did you get that photo?"

"Sure did. It's going through a face recognition query as we speak but there aren't enough points of comparison and that photo is grainy as shit. But I have a guy looking into that ink on his hand. Too bad it's just a partial. Got any extra footage for me?"

I wanted like hell to give it to her, but I couldn't. "It's best for all of us if no one else sees that image."

## HEAVENLY HACKED

Peaches went quiet, deadly so. "Damn girl, what are you into? I thought you didn't fuck with that black hat shit."

"I don't. It's just ... fucked up for now. I'm offline but you can find me in the usual ways."

"Stay safe, babe. Love ya."

"Back atcha, Peach."

If there was anyone in this world I considered a friend, it was Peaches. We met as cocky sixteen year olds with massive chips on our leather clad shoulders, assigned to do community service teaching old people how to use computers. She'd hacked into her girlfriend's computer, at least that was the story she told. The rest of the story, the real part, was that her girlfriend was the Deputy Headmistress of her private school. I was there for giving a few nasty bullies lower grades, but the school called it hacking. Semantics.

I needed to keep Peaches as clear of this as possible. Given what I saw at Jeremiah's place I probably shouldn't involve him either.

That meant I didn't need to stay in Vegas proper. I could find a more remote campsite. With privacy. And one exit.

The first thing I would do as soon as I got settled? Look into Jeremiah and his club.

Just in case.

# Chapter Three

*Jag*

"Your girl has brass balls man. Titanium. If she hadn't laid it all out like she did, we would've all been completely fucked."

All of us, the entire Reckless Bastards organization owed Rocky a debt of gratitude. She'd saved our asses and made sure none of our brothers left the world before their time.

"Anything she needs."

Lasso looked at me with a grateful but exhausted grin as he slumped in a cafeteria chair, his eyes going to the elevator every fifteen seconds since Rocky had kicked him out of the room for the next hour, demanding some privacy for herself and rest for him. "Rocky's not exactly the asking for help sort," he said with a snort and a laugh.

"Maybe not but she is pregnant as hell which means she's got disgusting midnight cravings, weird needs or whatever. Trust me, I learned more than I ever wanted to about the craziness of pregnant women. Mom spent years as a nurse in the maternity ward and she never spared me the details. Mom thought it was the best form of birth control."

That pulled a laugh from Lasso. "I'll be sure to let her know."

"No need. I'm just telling you because she's your woman. And because I don't think she'll cash in all that good will she deserves." If possible, Lasso had met a woman more stubborn than him. Rocky was smart as hell and twice as stubborn, which went against Lasso's natural tendency towards chivalry.

"Probably not but I'm not opposed to it." His blue gaze scanned the cafeteria. "Stitch all right?"

"Hell yeah. He's eating up all the attention from the Reckless Bitches, getting massages and sponge baths and shit. Eating it up." The kid had made it through a tour and a half in the desert without catching a bullet only to take one at a whorehouse on the outskirts of Las Vegas and he was giddy. "The bagged tacos for Rocky were from Stitch."

"Then why is it that it's my woman and baby hooked up to monitors upstairs but you look even more worried than me?"

Damn, I didn't realize I wasn't doing a good job of hiding my emotions. The past few days had drained me, physically and emotionally. The appearance of Vivi compounded everything to keep me uneasy and anxious as fuck. "Remember that girl I told you about? NextGen? She showed up the night the shit hit the fan."

Lasso let out a long, low whistle. "No shit? She say why?"

I shook my head because that was the motherfucker of it all, wasn't it? "Nope. I didn't give her a chance with all the shit going on that night but she left me her number." That had been a couple days ago, though. "She's probably long gone by now." I didn't know what to think about her just showing up. "I haven't talked to her in more than a decade."

That didn't mean Vivi was ever far from my thoughts, she wasn't. When Mom was killed, I wanted to reach out to her, let her help me with my grief but the sting of rejection combined with said grief had me doing the only thing an introverted loner could. I withdrew into myself. But I couldn't deny that when life was hard—basic training, my first tour, special ops—she was the first person I'd thought of and wondered about.

"I mean it is suspect that she showed up when she did but it sounds like a random fucked up coincidence. Are you gonna call her?"

"I have no clue, man. I mean between all the shit that went down and then seeing her for the first time ever in my whole fucking life it was like a fucking nuclear shock. I couldn't even fucking speak. My thoughts alternated between you and Rocky and why Vivi was on my doorstep. Even now I can't process her being *here*. In Vegas."

"Call her."

## HEAVENLY HACKED

"It's probably too late. She said she'd be in town for a couple days and that was two days ago."

Lasso shrugged and stood, his dry hospital cafeteria cheeseburger all but abandoned on the plastic tray. "Aren't you some bad ass computer hacker dude?"

"Allegedly." But the fact was that if Vivi had kept up with it, she was likely miles ahead of me in skill and talent. Even with my covert training. I sighed. "Maybe it's better if she's already gone."

We walked back to the elevators in silence, both of us lost in thought before Lasso finally spoke. "You know, if Rocky had thought I was some jerk who wouldn't care, she wouldn't have ended up on my door step and I wouldn't have her in my life now."

"You were always going to find a wife and make a bunch of ankle biters, man. That's what your big Texas ass was built for."

"Yours, too, even though you refuse to believe it. I'm happy to argue that with you another time but for now, something must be wrong for her to finally decide it was time to meet you in person. If you can turn your back on that, maybe you're not meant for those connections you hate so much."

I sighed. "I don't hate them, man. It's just that some people aren't built for that shit. Just look at the string of broken connections in my life for proof."

"Bullshit. I'm still here and so is Gunnar and the rest of the Bastards, which proves your little theory dead ass wrong. But that's okay, you do what you gotta do brother. I've got a pregnant wife to hover over until she screams with annoyance." He flashed a smile that told me exactly how much he loved it as he pushed inside the room. "Thanks for the food, clothes and company, man."

"Anytime, brother. Take care of our girl."

"Always."

I watched him go, smiling the moment his gaze landed on Rocky. Even though her hair was messy and she was pale and bruised, he looked at her like she was the beginning and end of his world. That was real, true, honest to goodness love. The kind that had been ripped from my own mother when my dad interrupted a junkie trying to stick up a convenience store and caught two in the chest for his efforts.

I'd leave that kind of shit to Lasso and the rest of the boys falling like dead weight into love with some pretty incredible women. But that didn't mean I'd leave Vivi to flounder on her own. If she needed my help I'd give it to her.

\*\*\*

"Not exactly what I pictured when you said you had a place to stay." After tracking her phone and then double-checking the data, I hopped on my bike and drove forty-five minutes outside the city to some rundown campsite filled with what looked like homeless people. People who no longer fit into society—along with those who didn't want to—set up their homes there.

I wondered what it said about Vivi that she had set up her brand-new camper there as well.

"What are you doing here Jeremiah?" She sounded annoyed but not surprised to see me.

"You gave me your number. It was easy." It took me less than five minutes to pinpoint her location.

She glared, her gray eyes hard and stormy. "It wasn't a challenge. When you didn't call me, I took the hint and moved on." She leaned against the open door. She'd stepped out when she heard me roar up outside her camper but I could tell she had a tight grip on the handle. Cautious and defensive. "So, what are you doing here?"

"I should be asking you that. What brings you to Vegas?"

She shrugged like it was nothing but Vivi couldn't hide the tension in her body for shit. "Just passing through."

Vague enough to be true but not nearly the entire story. "To where?"

## HEAVENLY HACKED

"Haven't decided yet. When I get on the road *soon,* I'll figure it out." She was being purposely vague. I didn't know if she was trying to see if she could trust me or she just didn't want to tell me.

"Where you coming from?"

"Back east. New York," she offered up, probably because it was easy enough to verify.

"And you decided to look me up because?"

She shrugged again and I was getting damn tired of that shrug. "You were on my mind when I hit Chicago and I did a little surfing and decided to finally get that face to face we never had." The words were incongruous for the woman standing in front of me. The black tank top and leather cuff watch screamed badass, but those gray eyes looked vulnerable. Wary. Even scared.

"Have lunch with me." Something was clearly going on with her. Her eyes glinted silver in the late morning sun as she looked me over. Her gaze was long and thorough but there was no heat behind it. No hate either so I guessed that was a good thing.

"Sure. When and where?"

A smile spread slowly across my face. "My day is free. I'll wait for you." It took all the restraint I had not to laugh at the way her jaws clenched at my answer.

She stared at me for a long moment, opened the door wider and sighed. "Fine. Come inside and don't touch any of my shit."

I took a seat at the smallest goddamn dinette I'd ever seen, barely able to move to look around. "Other than the fact I'm stuck in this tiny thing, I won't touch a thing." She laughed, and I took my time checking her out.

I'd imagined her a thousand times over the years. I imagined her Asian most of the time, with colored hair and maybe a few piercings. But the blue hair wasn't bad, neither was the pale freckled skin or the sleeve of tattoos. It was sexy as hell. *She* was sexy as hell, in a slightly sarcastic and annoyed way. "This thing looks new."

"It is," she said behind a half closed door that looked like a bedroom. "Cheaper than a decent hotel and easier to check out." Her words were light but she couldn't hide the tension in every syllable.

"Sounds like you're on the run from something."

"Yeah well it seems like maybe you should've been when I rolled into town." She stopped at the table, giving me a good long look at her tits. They were perfect. Perky. "Get a good look?"

My eyes crawled up her body until they got to her face. "Not good enough but it'll hold. For now." I gave in to the impulse to finish my perusal of her body because I needed a good close look at her shapely legs. She wore jeans that had to be painted on because I could see every muscle, every dip and curve. Up close they were even better. They slid into... "Cowboy boots?"

"They're cute and comfortable. Breathable in this heat. Let's go."

"No tour?" I stood, towering over her with a smile. Vivi was definitely tough but she clearly still spent too much time on her own because she had a shitty poker face. And she couldn't hide the fluttering pulse at the base of her throat.

"Come on, playa."

The laugh erupted before I could do anything to stop it. "Vivi, that shit is right up there with homie."

She sucked in a breath as the memory came to her. "I am the hippest chick on the planet, thank you very much."

"I'll let that one slide only because you let me look at your tits."

"I wouldn't say *let*, you dirty old man."

I laughed. "Aren't you like three months older than me? That makes you a cougar."

She waved me out of the camper and locked the side door. "Give me the address and I'll meet you there."

## HEAVENLY HACKED

"I don't think so, babe. Hop on the back of my bike." I smiled and looked around the campsite. "Where's your bike?"

"Someplace safe. And I don't take rides from strangers."

"Fine. Mayhem Diner. See you there." I wasn't worried. I knew she would show because she knew I would track her down. Again. And again if I had to. And five minutes after I took a seat, she walked in with attitude radiating off her in waves.

"Vivi. So glad you could join me."

She flashed a fake ass smile as she—reluctantly—took the seat that put her back facing the door. More proof that she was in some deep shit. "Jeremiah. You made me drive that big ass camper over here so tell me, what's up?"

So we were gonna do small talk. "Quite a lot, actually. But nothing you really care about."

43

She opened her mouth to say something bitchy I'm sure, but our waitress Myrna stopped to take our order. "What can I getcha?"

"I'll have the garden salad and a cheeseburger with grilled onions. A tall glass of ice water and an iced tea, please."

"A girl with an appetite and a figure like that? Where'd you find this one, Jag?"

"She found me, Myrna."

"Smart girl," she said and flashed a wink at Vivi. "What'll it be, Jag?"

"Steak sandwich and fries. Extra cheese. Thanks."

"No problem. I'll be back with your drinks." She winked one last time, always trying to play the role of matchmaker.

"Don't mind, Myrna. She thinks we're all her children. She's sweet and firm, always has a piece of advice you didn't ask for but needed anyway."

"You like her."

## HEAVENLY HACKED

"She's great." Myrna brought the drinks and Vivi took her time, arranging both glasses until they were perfect. She was hesitating. "Vivi you sought me out. Why?"

She sighed and took a long sip of her iced tea. Under the harsh diner lights the colors and shadows of her tattoos looked ominous. Foreboding. She didn't want to answer. Either that or she was trying to figure out which version of the truth to tell me. "Like I said, I was curious."

"You never were before."

She winced at my tone, nodding absently. "I figured that's how you saw it even though it's not the truth. Doesn't matter now, though, does it?"

"How else should I have seen it?" If she didn't want to talk about why she'd come here, then she could tell me why she didn't want to meet with me so many years ago.

"Maybe you should have considered that I was all on my own and worried about everything. I was worried you wouldn't like me because I was flat-chested and I had shitty clothes. My place didn't have much furniture, just a big ass sofa, a TV and plenty of computer equipment. I was embarrassed and afraid."

"Here you kids go." Myrna's appearance with the food did nothing to break the tension.

"You're right, I probably should have realized all that. I didn't."

"Of course you didn't. You were a kid too. We were just too damn smart to realize how little we knew." One side of her pink mouth curled into a grin. "Anyway, I'm sorry Jeremiah. You were my only friend for a long time and you deserved better."

What was I supposed to say to return the sentiment? I shrugged because it was all I could do in that moment. Maybe I did owe her some type of apology but I wasn't ready to forget the rejection I felt at her hands. "Vivi I know you're in trouble. If you want my help, tell me."

# HEAVENLY HACKED

She nodded around her burger. "I'm still trying to decide if I need your help."

At least she was honest. "I don't have time for games. Either you want my help or you don't." I should have known it wasn't the right way to go about things with her. Vivi had always been prickly and I imagined her life hadn't done much to change that.

Her demeanor changed in an instant. There was tension coiled tightly through every inch of her as she slowly nodded her head. She moved in deliberate moves as she picked up the napkin and wiped her mouth before dropping it beside the plate. "Good to know." Her words were quiet. Deadly cool as she stood and dropped a fifty on the table. "See you around. Jag."

I had to smile at her as she walked away and not just because of the fine ass swaying back and forth but because of the dig. She'd used my given name before because that was how she knew me. Now, she didn't know me at all.

Or so she thought.

Vivi had showed up in my life for a reason and I would find out.

One way or another.

## Chapter Four

*Vivi*

Lunch with Jeremiah reminded me why I kept my profile low and my life solitary for the most part. People were unreliable. Just when you thought you knew someone, they did something to betray you or, if you were lucky, just reminded you that people couldn't be trusted. In the case of Jeremiah—now *Jag*—they changed altogether.

It didn't matter. In the end he'd done me a favor by reminding me that I was much better on my own. I returned to my campsite and then moved to another one before I got back to work. Digging into the encrypted data that had started this mess was the first step to trying to end it.

I'd found a few things that I wasn't looking for the first time around, starting with the name of the asset. Some of the file creator data called him Jonas but that was likely an alias. As I went back through the backups of backups I went back to the photos. Five in total, two were of Governor Blaise and Angela, his seventeen-year-old girlfriend. They were holding hands in one and she was straddling his hips as they made out passionately on the beach in Miami in the other. My money was on Blaise because he was deep into his second term and people were already whispering the one word that would make these photos a dream killer.

POTUS.

The other three photos were clearly of a gangster. If not because of his Italian last name then because of the leather vest he wore and the bandana around the lower half of his face. In all three photos he was with the same two men in suits, definitely federal agents. They were in a park in one, a diner in another and outside a cheap motel in the final picture. It was pretty obvious the man was an informant.

Whoever it was, I was clearly fucked six ways from Sunday because none of it made sense. Most of the data, especially the photos, were out of context, and assuming someone knew Jonas—whoever the fuck *he* was—they still had a lot of damn dots to connect before they got to me. That was why I figured Blaise had done it; he might have access to someone with access to the right information.

Either that—or Bob was dirty.

Digging into any politician was dangerous, simply because I never knew who else I might run into while searching. But there was also the whole criminal act part that I had to ignore because survival was my top priority. Blaise made it easy to dig into him because his work and personal devices were one and the same. One laptop. One phone. One tablet. He had a great security set-up, most government agencies thought they were invulnerable, but hacking into his shit was easy for a geek like me.

That made it easy to find everything he tried to wipe and a few things he probably thought no one would ever discover. There was a bigger skeleton than his young side piece, so I uploaded everything I had on him to several different sources because backups came in handy when dealing with shady motherfuckers.

And this lying, cheating cradle-robber was the shadiest of them all.

I hesitated for a few minutes on whether or not I should send the other photo to Peaches. She was already too involved. But identifying this guy could tell me who was after me. Maybe. Hopefully.

I decided to sit on it for now while I did more digging into Blaise. He had so much more to lose and a greater need to keep his distance from any whiff of scandal. I needed to find evidence of payments to an individual or company in the last few weeks, but financial records were a bitch to access. It was even worse with banks outside the US and in particular with those financial institutions located in places that helped the rich people hide their money.

But it was a necessary step so I put on a pot of coffee, grabbed a bag of pretzels, some mustard for dipping, and got down to work. It took me hours to find no trace of a payment to anyone or anything suspicious. Dammit.

# HEAVENLY HACKED

That was the downside of my job. I could spend sixteen hours sitting in front of a computer, digging and coding and still wind up with absolutely nothing. It was frustrating as hell but it was also the nature of the beast.

A knock startled the shit out of me and instinctively, I reached for my knife. It was a six-inch blade with one serrated edge and spring-loaded hinges. Perfect for personal protection. I gripped the handle and took several deep breaths to clear my mind. If I needed to fight or defend myself, then I needed to be calm. Rational. That was hard to do when I slid open the small window on the door and caught a glimpse of my visitor. "What are you doing here?"

Jeremiah grinned like he was some adorable schoolboy instead of a grown ass man with big sexy muscles. "I was in the area and thought I'd stop by. Bad time?"

"Yep. Maybe next time pick up the phone." I didn't like unexpected visitors and I liked them even less when someone was out to get me.

"I tried that but you never answer and you don't call back."

He wore a smirk that I shouldn't have found sexy, but I did. I so, so did. That was another very good reason to keep myself on one side of the door and Jeremiah on the other.

"Why?" he asked

"I realized you were right. I don't need anyone else's help and I'm perfectly capable of handling things on my own. So, thank you Jeremiah. And it was good to meet you. Finally."

I gave him one last look and shut the door. No matter what happened, I was sure I'd never see Jeremiah again.

# Chapter Five

*Jag*

My hand was balled into a fist as I pounded on the door again. "It's real cute you thought you could get rid of me so easily, Vivi." Why in the hell did I make this long ass drive anyway? She clearly wasn't going to tell me the truth and I didn't have the time or energy to deal with this bullshit.

"Go away!" Her voice came from deeper inside the camper now, which meant she was comfortable.

"Come on, Vivi. You came all the way to Vegas to get a look at my pretty face, get your ass out here and let's catch up." I walked away from the camper, toward two chairs set up to look at the stars. She was stubborn as hell but the girl I remembered just needed to cool down and she would be okay.

When the door opened I grinned to myself. When she dropped into the chair beside me with a bag of pretzels in one hand and a bottle of root beer in the other, my smile grew bigger.

"Why did you come here, Jeremiah?"

"Call me Jag."

She popped a pretzel stick into her mouth. "Why?"

"Because I'm sexy as hell and as smooth and stealthy as a jaguar." She laughed at the answer, shaking her head. When she looked at me I could still see disbelief shining in her eyes. "I can't believe we're here like this. You and your root beer and pretzels."

She sucked in a breath and pointed at me. "Don't do that."

"Fine." I held my hands up defensively but I couldn't stop smiling and it ruined the effect. "What are you up to these days?"

"Cyber security, what else?"

"Right, but how'd it all come about? Christ, woman it's called a conversation." It was never this

## HEAVENLY HACKED

hard to start a conversation with Vivi. Maybe she was one of those people who felt more comfortable hiding behind a computer screen. I hoped so because the alternative was that life had fucked her over and she didn't open up to anyone. At all.

"I did a few of those tech competitions with the fat paychecks and placed in the top three, which sent all the government and corporate scum suckers to my front door to offer me money to break their systems. One contract turned into two and so on and so forth." She said it all so nonchalantly, like it wasn't a big damn deal when it was.

"Damn. That's great."

"I guess. What about you? From soldier to outlaw biker?"

I couldn't take my eyes off her. Sure, she was hot as fuck, but it wasn't that. Well, it wasn't *just* that. It was surreal, sitting under the stars with the girl who'd been my best friend growing up. "Not so much an outlaw. Our businesses are all legal. Mostly."

She laughed and that sound was like a kick in the gut. We may have never met in real life but her laugh was bliss. "It's good to see you Jeremiah."

"Your laugh has saved my life on plenty of occasions, Genevieve." It was a stupid thing to say and based on her shocked look, I'd probably freaked her the fuck out.

"Don't call me that. And I'm glad you didn't get yourself killed over there."

"Gee thanks *Vivi*." And just like that I was the blushing teenager again.

"So, how'd you end up a…what's it called again? A Reckless Bastard?"

This was it, the real test of the strength of our old friendship. Did I tell her the truth or did I give her the bullshit answer people wanted to hear when they asked personal questions? "Honestly? I kind of fell into it."

She laughed because it sounded crazy as hell. I knew that. "I spent most of my military career doing covert shit I can't talk about. Ever. It was a hard way to live but I found a bright spot and her name was Kendall. We fell in love in that fucking hellhole. She was a medic assigned to the unit and we had eighteen months together before she got killed when an RPG took down the chopper."

"Oh shit, Jeremiah. I'm sorry." Her face didn't hold the same phony sympathy I was used to seeing, probably because she knew it was one more loss for me.

"Anyway I was fucked up when I was discharged. Spending days in Silicon Valley, going where the government dispatched me to offer my expertise on the latest war tech and I spent my nights drinking. One night there was this big motherfucker getting drunker than me. He looked worse than me, too, and some guys were giving him shit."

"Jeremiah to the rescue?"

"Something like that," I grinned at her. "He could've fucked them up if he wanted to, but he was punishing himself, I could tell. So I intervened before anyone got really hurt. That big fucker was Gunner, our VP." Me and Gunnar, we saved each other from our grief and in the process became brothers. "Lasso came to retrieve him a few days later and the rest is history."

She smiled and swigged on her root beer. "I'm glad you have them, then."

"What about you, who do you have now?" It wasn't the slickest way to ask if she was seeing anyone but then, I never claimed to be slick.

"I have me and that's all I need."

"Dammit, Vivi. Come on, just talk to me. You're here now, just say what you have to say."

She stood angrily. "I didn't realize it was such a problem that I tracked you down, *Jag*. Believe me when I say I won't be making that mistake again." She bent over to pick up the discarded bottle, giving me another long look at her ass.

"I didn't mean it like that, girl."

"It's fine. Don't worry about me. It was just a temporary bout of insanity, that's all. Take care of yourself." She turned away quickly, this time but she held herself tall. Strong. Dignified.

## HEAVENLY HACKED

"I'm sorry, Vivi. I want to help you if I can."

"You can't. But thanks."

This was getting damned frustrating. "Then why in the hell did you track me down if you didn't want my help? Or don't even want to talk to me?"

She sighed and turned around inside the doorway of the camper, her pose highlighting her body magnificently. "I thought maybe you could help me, Jeremiah. But we're different people now, a fact that only occurred to me after I got here." Another annoyed sigh exploded out of her and she raked a hand through her wild blue hair. "I'm sorry I interrupted your life."

She disappeared inside the camper and she didn't come back out again, effectively dismissing me.

"You could have offered me a root beer!" I tossed back at her as I walked toward my bike.

I would go, for tonight. But this wasn't over. She needed my help and she would get it.

# Chapter Six

*Vivi*

The sun hadn't even come up yet when one of the ten thousand alarms set up on my phone started to blare. Literally it blared right in my fucking ear. The foghorn sound I'd assigned to…"Shit!" I sat up in the tiny ass bed and promptly fell to the floor, reaching on the bed for the offensive sound that meant someone was in my New York apartment. Again.

The video feed showed a man. Tall and white and bald with a tattoo on the top of his wrist very similar to the other intruder's. If it wasn't the same person, they were definitely from the same criminal organization. He was sloppy though, not as professional as the other guy. Bald Head was clearly a hired thug, the way he stomped through the place, overturning pillows unnecessarily and displacing lamps. It wasn't just careless, it was also stupid as hell because he left fingerprints and DNA everywhere. On top of all that, the asshole was too late.

The decoy electronics were already gone which meant it was time for extreme measures. Measures I'd put in place when I first bought that place a few years ago because deep down every hacker knows this is likely to happen to them. The smart ones, like me, are prepared for the worst. And though it physically hurt me to do it, I flipped the kill switch that activated magnetic strips placed throughout the unit, effectively killing all digital devices that crossed them. Including the intruder's cell phone, a fact which gave me the delight of a three year old eating chocolate ice cream for breakfast, as I watched him try in vain to make call after call.

The deadbolt locks engaged on the doors and windows, leaving him trapped inside while the silent alarm triggered the police who would be sent the code to disarm everything. On site. He was fucked and even though it meant I wouldn't get any information from him, I was glad someone would pay for something.

# HEAVENLY HACKED

The appearance of this bald guy really threw me, though, because it seemed like two separate attacks. Two different intruders. "Whoever you are, you should have done your homework, asshole." It brought me entirely too much enjoyment to see him running around my place in search of an exit, but nothing topped his expression when he heard the sirens. It was always a good day when I found something that made me smile, at least that was what my shrink used to tell me.

A noise outside drew my attention and I muted the video feed while I stood slowly, eyes closed to hear where exactly the sound had originated. My fender faced the road and I was situated on a dead end road to make sure I could hear any cars drive up and I hadn't heard any. Then I heard it, the snap of the twigs I'd spread around the camper for just that purpose, so I grabbed my knife.

The side window on the driver's side slid open and I tiptoed over, grabbing the cotton covered arm that had invaded my space. "Think real carefully about your next move, asshole. If I don't like what you have to say, I'll split this vein open and watch you bleed out before you get your arm away from me."

"I knew you were in trouble." That voice was familiar. Too fucking familiar.

"Jeremiah? What the fuck?" I wasn't in the mood for his games and last night he made me feel like shit for reaching out to him, making me regret that the idea had ever occurred to me in the first place. "Why are you here?"

"I told you to call me Jag." I could hear the smile in his deep voice and it only pissed me off even more.

"It's a stupid name and I don't plan on calling you anything."

He chuckled and I wanted to prick him with the tip of my knife, just because I could. "Can I have my arm back?"

"That depends. What are you doing skulking around my shit at this hour?"

## HEAVENLY HACKED

"What the hell do you think, Vivi? You show up, out of the blue and clearly in trouble that you won't tell me about. I came to see just how bad it was and now I have my answer."

I released his arm, closing and locking the window behind him. The man was a stubborn damn jackass who clearly didn't know how to take 'no' for an answer. "I told you as much as I'm going to, *Jag*. If I need your help then *I* will call *you*. Got it?" The metal door was open but the screen door stood closed between us.

"I want to help. Let me." Jeremiah pushed up onto the next step and opened the door, invading my space.

I snorted at the ridiculousness of his statement. "It looks like you have your own mess going on based on what I saw."

"What can I say, I'm good at multi-tasking." He stepped closer, until I had no choice but to touch him intimately or back down. I *never* backed down. One hand shot to my waist, his thumb dragging against the exposed skin at my waistband. "See, I'm helpful."

I laughed and pushed at his chest, but Jeremiah was all man and he didn't budge. He stared at me and I stared back, feeling my blood heat at all the energy swirling in the air between us. The charge of electricity made the camper feel ten degrees hotter. His expression was serious as he closed in, mouth descending on mine slowly, giving me time to decide if it would happen.

Luckily Jeremiah had no clue as to the effect he was having on me, didn't know there was no choice because then I'd be in real trouble. Now the only danger I was in was having my clothes burst into flames from his nearness, from the deliciously hot way his full lips pressed against mine. From the taste of him, sugar and coffee and something earthy. Sexy. Masculine. The kiss was hot and hard, filled with hunger and raw unabashed need. Big hands cupped my ass and then my breasts. Something long and hard pressed against my belly and I pulled back, panting and staring at him with wide eyes. "What was that?"

## HEAVENLY HACKED

With sleepy eyes and a captivating fucking smile he leaned in and brushed his lips against my neck. "If I have to tell you, then I'm doing it wrong babe."

I laughed and shook my head. "If you'd done it any more right I'd be naked and wrapped around you right now. But why?"

"Why not," he shrugged like it made perfect sense. "You're hot as fuck and you've always turned me on when you were so damn prickly, which apparently, is all the damn time."

I spluttered in my outrage and the jerk only laughed harder at me. "Asshole."

"Meet me at the diner tomorrow for breakfast. Eight o'clock sharp. This place is too fucking far."

"Yeah well no one invited you up here." It was something to say but the amused look he gave me told me it was a lost cause.

His dark gaze was serious. And seriously hot. "Don't make me come back up here, Vivi." His words were a warning. A promise.

And for some reason it sounded good. Right. Hot. Sexy.

*** 

I really wasn't in the mood to get up at the ass crack of dawn to meet Jag, but I knew if I didn't then he'd come up here and invade my space. Again. But meeting him at the diner meant either leaving my camper and my gear behind or taking this big bitch back on the road.

Since I would never leave my surveillance equipment behind, I took my time getting dressed and guzzling a pot of coffee before I got on the road. Going approximately fifty miles an hour gave me plenty of time to think about what I'd wanted to happen with Jeremiah. Or *Jag*, because that was what I needed to get used to calling him. I needed to just talk to him about what I needed from him. No more games and no more bullshit. It didn't matter that he wasn't the boy I knew online anymore, what mattered was that he had the skills I needed to get out of this shit storm.

## HEAVENLY HACKED

Like the beige sedan that had been trailing me for the past eight miles. It was an older model by at least twenty years given how boxy the body was and the driver kept two car lengths between us, a by-the-book tail. I didn't do anything differently, anything that might indicate he'd been made. I took the Mayhem exit and found one of several public parking lots in town to park, keeping a close eye on the beige heap of junk.

The car didn't park though, instead he waited for me to get out and start my journey. I grabbed my bag, engaged the booby traps and locks on the camper, then stepped out onto what was basically Main Street in Mayhem and walked towards the delicious greasy smells of the diner.

The diner was located in the middle of the block, which meant the scrap of metal had to slowly chug along the street and draw attention to itself.

The jerk chose to follow me closely so I ducked into a book store and waited five minutes before slipping back out like nothing was going on. When I arrived at the diner, I was ten minutes late and Jag looked suitably annoyed.

"You're late," he said as soon as I slid into the booth with my back to the door.

"You're lucky I'm here at all." I flipped over the coffee cup and set it as close to the edge of the table as possible to encourage the busy waitress to fill me up. "Look outside and tell me if you see a late model beige sedan. It's been following me since about five miles from the campsite."

Jag's black brows rose, and I knew what he was thinking before he said the words. "You sure?"

"Just look outside and tell me if you see the car, Jag."

Everything about him said he thought I was batshit fucking crazy. Until he spotted the car. His brows rose and velvety brown eyes grew as wide as the pancakes just set down in front of him. "I see it. Can't see inside because of the glare, though."

## HEAVENLY HACKED

"Doesn't matter. He's a middle-aged, nondescript white male. As run of the mill as they come." The guy was probably a pro. A pro what? I had no fucking idea and didn't care. I just wanted to be left the hell alone. "So what was so urgent we had to meet for breakfast before the roosters woke up?"

A grin split his face and he looked at me with something like affection in his eyes. I ignored the feelings it caused and waited. "You wanted to speak with me," he clarified.

"Wrong. I thought I did and I changed my mind, so you offered to buy me breakfast to get me to change my mind." I stabbed the potatoes with my fork and shoved them into my mouth with a smile.

"And are you ready to talk yet or do I need to pile on the charm?"

I laughed and shook my head. "Save the charm for someone else, Jag. I'm only interested in your help. A very specific kind of help so I'll tell you enough to let you decide if you are willing and able to help." I took a long sip of coffee until the steaming black liquid burned my insides and then I told him my story. A story light on details but with enough flesh that he got the gist of my predicament. "So there you have it, the whole sordid tale."

Jag's expression was blank as he stared at me for longer than I felt comfortable letting him stare, but eventually his shoulders relaxed, and he seemed calm. "You have my help. Whatever you need, say the word."

That was exactly what I wanted to hear but I wasn't satisfied. "I'm happy to hear that but it seems like you and your people have enough going on and the last thing I need right now is for any kind of law enforcement to interfere in my life."

"Why don't you let me worry about that?" His smile was playful and boyish. Irresistible. "Now that I'm helping, do I get all the details?"

"Not here in the open." I couldn't take the chance that I was being followed by someone else that I hadn't seen and have them overhear what I knew for certain. "What was going on when I pulled up to your…place?"

## HEAVENLY HACKED

He grinned again, something that came easily to him. I envied that, his ability to wear a smile no matter what was happening. "Some asshole thought he could order his ex to come back to him by threatening her. We had to show him he was wrong. Plus, that ex is my buddy's wife now."

"Shit." That was some serious shit. "And that little lesson required all the emergency vehicles in town? I call bullshit, but you don't have to tell me if you don't want to." It was probably best if we kept some secrets between us.

"I just told you. Rocky used to date this scumbag who was the head of a gang in LA and when his business started going south he decided he wanted her particular brand of assistance again. He wouldn't take no for an answer and me and my brothers had to say it until he heard it and accepted it."

The way my body reacted to his words, so calm and harsh with a deadly dose of venom running through his tone, was crazy. It felt crazy and out of control, like I was setting back the women's movement at least a hundred years. But I was turned on by his words, the certainty in them and the ferocity with which he spoke them. "So you're like a real-life outlaw biker, huh?"

"A biker yes but we're not outlaws. Not really," he added hastily. "We have legit businesses that we all run and yeah, if someone fucks with one of us, they fuck with us all."

"Good to know." I could still catch glimpses of the boy I used to know, especially when he said certain phrases or laughed. God, that laugh had been the balm my battered heart and soul longed for back then. It was rich and loud, full of life and enjoyment. Jeremiah was a boy who'd enjoyed life, at least until it had all been snatched from him. I still hadn't decided if I would accept the help he offered but I was glad we'd gotten a chance to talk for a bit, so I dropped some cash in the tray with the check, passing on the mints, and handed it to the passing waitress. "This was fun, Jag."

He frowned and looked up at me. "That's the second time you bought me a meal and I don't like it."

# HEAVENLY HACKED

It was almost a pout, a sexy little pout that made me think about kissing him again. Dammit.

"Don't worry, I fully expect you to put out." A laugh escaped at his shocked expression.

"I can do that. But first we should probably talk about things, don't you think Vivi?"

Hell no I didn't think we needed to talk about anything, especially when he pitched his voice low and panty meltingly sexy. "I'll let you know."

Jag stood and got in my face. "You can follow me to my place."

I could have argued and told him that no one bossed me around and then went on about my way. But I was too damn curious about him and those kissable fucking lips so I nodded and left the diner because I was about to do something really stupid.

Like sleep with Jag.

## Chapter Seven

*Jag*

Whatever shit Vivi had gotten herself into was deep enough to get her to come to me after more than a decade of radio silence. I was sure the way I pulled away from her years ago had a lot to do with why she was so damn prickly right now. Still, she didn't turn the other way at her first chance. Instead, she followed behind until we reached the outskirts of town and pulled into the plot of land I bought a few years ago. It wasn't much but it had plenty of space for a house, a computer lab and a garage for all my vehicles. It was all mine and that's what mattered to me.

"Go on into the garage and kill the engine," I told her, stopping my bike just outside the entrance.

"Aye, captain." She gave a sarcastic salute and managed to squeeze her camper into the small space without my help.

"What do you want help with first?" I stood in the back doorway with my arms crossed, staring at her as she stared back at me, gray eyes liquid and sharp.

"I don't need help with anything. That's the point of having a camper so I don't have to unpack my shit everywhere I go. Come in."

I followed her to the dinette and she patted the seat beside her, fingers already flying across the keyboard quick enough to leave a dust trail. "I know you're eager to see what brought me to your door."

She wasn't wrong about that, so I sat next to her and tried like hell to ignore the scent of vanilla that swamped me as soon as I got close to her. Vanilla and something else, earthy and musky and sexy as fuck. I slid away to put some space between us. "Let's see what you got."

She rolled her eyes, which looked like melted silver up close against the backdrop of her electric blue hair and pulled up two images. "That," she pointed, and I leaned in to see two photos both of a vaguely familiar looking white dude with a young chick who wasn't nearly as polished or vanilla enough to be his wife.

It didn't appear all that nefarious to me and I leaned back with a sigh. "That's it? A rich white guy cheating on his wife isn't exactly a big scandal worthy of all this cloak and dagger stuff. Is it?" Then another thought occurred to me, *what if Vivi was crazy?*

She sighed. "I should have known," she grumbled and shut the laptop harder than she needed to. "Men. Don't worry about it, Jag. I have a few things I need to take care of here, but I'll be gone in an hour or so."

"Goddamnit woman, you are as infuriating as fuck!" I smacked my hands on the table hard enough to jumble all the contents on top. "Stop being so fucking sensitive and don't run away from me again."

She slid her hips into mine until I stood to let her escape and she began to pace in the small camper. "Of course you don't see anything wrong about a grown man fucking a child. A child, Jag! She's a teenager, not just your run of the mill side piece!" The look she levelled me with made me feel about two feet tall.

Shit. "How in the hell was I supposed to know that?"

"Maybe don't be so quick to brush me off?" She held up her hands to stop me. "If you don't believe me or think I'm some paranoid nutjob, say so and I'll go. No harm, no foul and no complaints." Vivi stared at me with fire burning in her eyes, ready to bolt if I said the wrong thing. "Well?"

"I'm not saying I don't believe you, Vivi. Shit, you barely tell me anything and I'm just trying to figure this out."

She scoffed and shook her head, blue waves brushing her shoulders. "Figure this out Jag, she's seventeen today and they've been together for more than two years. Does that sink in? Or about the fact that the older guy in the photo is a politician. A governor to be exact."

I let out a shocked whistle because that piece of information was unexpected. "How exactly did you come across this information, Vivi? Are you doing black hat shit?"

## HEAVENLY HACKED

"No. It was a legitimate job that I can't tell you about and even if it had been black hat shit, I found the information, and someone is after me. So, can I trust you?"

I opened my mouth to tell her that she could trust me. I was a trustworthy sort of guy, ask anyone. But something stopped me. Vivi could trust me but only if she believed it. "Not if you think trust means following you blindly."

"If I needed a minion I could've stayed back east. I need someone with skills. I need to find out who is after me and how they found out about me." She told me about the break-in at her place that had prompted her to leave town and seek me out, so no matter what, Vivi believed someone was after her.

"Okay fine, you have my help. But I have a question. Why in hell would the government help him out if he's a child molester?" She didn't say it, but it didn't take a genius to figure out that her skills were perfect for multiple clandestine government agencies.

"I didn't say the whole government did this, but clearly he has a source or two. Or he knows someone who does."

"And you really think they'd kill over this?"

She scoffed and looked at me like I was poor dumb kid. "Let's see, the millions to be made as a crooked politician might be worth killing for. And how about a life in prison for sex with a child? Or maybe, and here's the kicker, maybe the idea of losing out on the Presidency. People have killed for less. A lot fucking less, Jag."

Her pointed words served as a reminder of what was going down with the Reckless Bastards when she rolled into town. "Point taken. Unless you're going to use this as an excuse to run away again?" She'd threatened to leave at least half a dozen times since she came to town and I didn't think she was playing games.

"That's because I'm the only person I can rely on, but I do need your help. But don't say you want to help just to keep me here, Jag. I'm not that girl and I don't need your protection."

## HEAVENLY HACKED

"You wouldn't take it even if you did need it." My lips curved into a smile because damn, Vivi was feisty as hell and it turned me on. "Right?"

Vivi fisted her hands at her hips, drawing my eyes to the beaded nipples peeking through the plain white tee she wore. I couldn't tell if she wore a bra or not, but her nipples were so hard I didn't give a damn. "I'm stubborn Jag, not stupid."

"Good to know. I'll remind you of that if I need to." I stood and got in her face, for no other reason than I could. She pushed at my chest when I got too close and I took a step back and I realized something. Vivi wasn't as immune to me as she pretended to be. Her pupils dilated and the pulse at the base of her neck fluttered wildly like a hummingbird's wings under her pale, silky flesh. I stepped in again and she pushed me back, but this time I didn't budge. One hand went to the back of her neck, massaging it at first until my fingers tangled in her hair, grabbing her to angle her head just so.

"Jag," she whispered a second before my mouth crashed down on hers in a frenzied kiss that felt like it had been twenty years in the making. My tongue swept against hers softly but the minx nipped my bottom lip, changing what would have been a sensual kiss into something hotter and darker. Something explosive.

Vivi's hand slid under my shirt, hands splayed wide as they traveled up my abdomen to my chest, taking the shirt as she rounded my shoulders.

"I guess we're taking this off," I whispered.

She nodded and leaned in, her tongue leaving a trail of heat up the center of my body. My cock sprang to life and she felt it, letting out a low moan as her tongue traveled to my nipple.

"Damn you are beautiful." She said the words more to herself than to me, but they slithered through my veins and lit a fire.

"Vivi." My voice came out a growl as her tongue curled around my other nipple while her fingers dug into my ass cheeks. She was as bossy right now as she'd been online, but I wasn't a shy boy anymore. "Vivi," I growled again, gripping a handful of blue hair to yank her back.

"Bedroom is up." She pointed to a fucking doll's bed and I shook my head.

"I don't fucking think so, Vivi." I knelt down and scooped her over my shoulder because there was no fucking way I was going to be smashed between a clear hatch and tiny ass bed the first time I slid into her. The garage was close to my bedroom and I had her naked and laid out on my bed in under two minutes. "That's better."

"Much fucking better," she said with a sexy smile as she propped up on her elbows to watch me undress. "I approve. Keep going."

A laugh escaped my burning lips but I kept my moves slow and deliberate. My shirt was still on the table in her camper so I kicked off my shoes as my hands went to my belt.

"For fuck's sake Jeremiah!"

Another laugh erupted out of me at her outraged tone but when Vivi fell back against the bed, her fingers slid between her thighs, exposing a swollen pink pussy, glistening with her juices. Pulsing and aching for me, I just knew it. I groaned and reached for her ankle, my pants forgotten in my need to taste her. To make her moan. To bring this bad ass woman to her knees. "You want something, Vivi?"

She nodded, her gaze transfixed by the sight of my dark hand crawling up her pale thigh and I couldn't deny the sight was amazing. The stark contrast making my cock harder. I gripped her thighs and pulled her to the edge of the bed, making her gasp. "Yeah. You."

I dove between her thighs, licking her slick pussy like I was a starving man and she was my last fucking meal. Sweet and sticky, tangy and tasty as fuck, I licked her, I sucked her, and my tongue fucked her until she was moaning and crying, writhing and bucking under me. I loved a responsive woman and Vivi's voice and body told me everything I did was right.

# HEAVENLY HACKED

When her hands palmed my head and pushed me against her as she pushed herself into my mouth, I sank one finger in slowly and sucked her clit. "Oh fuck, fuck! Fuck, Jeremiah!"

There was something so fucking satisfying hearing her call out my given name as she fell apart, convulsing and clenching around my finger as she rubbed her pussy all over me. I kept sucking her clit, slow and long to draw out her orgasm.

Waiting for her to surrender.

She came twice more before she did. "Okay! Fucking hell, okay!" I kept going until I heard the magic word. "Please. Fuck!"

I chuckled and stood up, staring at her flushed skin and heaving chest. I caught a flash of vibrant purples and blues on her left hip and cocked an eyebrow. "What's the tat?"

She rolled her eyes. "Less talking, more getting naked." We stared at each other for a long time until I gave in, unzipping my pants and pushing them to the floor. "It's a Phoenix's tail."

It was appropriate. She was indestructible, rising from the wreckage of those trying to burn her down. But I was done with questions about anything other than how she wanted me to fuck her as I climbed on the bed. "I'll check it out more carefully later."

"Good idea," she whispered and wrapped her legs around me as my cock sank into her wet pussy. "Yes," she hissed slowly until I was balls deep.

It felt so fucking good I just knelt there, weight on my hands to let the feel of her sink in. Hot as hell, tight as fuck and wet enough for a good fuck, Vivi's pink pussy was perfect. And impatient. She dug her heels into my ass and I pulled out and then slammed in. "Shit you're so tight."

"I use small vibrators," she said with a smirk.

"Smart ass." She was a smart ass and I knew exactly how to stop the next comment forming on those soft red lips. Vivi seemed like a woman who loved a good hard fuck. The harder I fucked her, the louder she screamed, the wetter her pussy grew and the harder it squeezed me.

"Oh shit! Yes!" She hung on as I thrusted into her like a man on a mission. What the mission was I had no fucking clue, all I knew was that her pussy felt too good to stop and when she came again, I didn't stop.

My cock wouldn't listen to reason, pounding hard and deep. Slow and deep. Fast and deep, my cock couldn't get enough of Vivi. Not when she came the second time and I put her ankles on my shoulder. Not when I fucked her so good she came all over my cock and my bed. "Vivi," I told her in a warning and she squeezed me tighter. "Fuck."

"Yes. Fuck me. Harder."

My control snapped and I reared up on my knees, spreading her wide so I could watch as my cock disappeared into her swollen pink opening. Over and over, I was hypnotized by the move until my spine began to tingle and my balls grew tight. "Viv," I groaned and leaned over so our bodies were smashed together.

"You're close. I can feel how hard you just got," she whispered as my hips moved faster and faster. The rush of liquid from her body so hot and slick I couldn't hold out any longer and my orgasm shot out of my body in a violent convulsion that shook the whole bed.

"Oh fuck, Viv." Her pussy pulsed at the way I said her name. "Shit," I whimpered, every muscle turned to rubber as I collapsed into her neck.

She laughed. "Don't think that sex, no matter how amazing, will distract me from what I need to do."

I managed to lift my head. I didn't think it would, but she didn't need to know that. "Amazing, huh?"

She rolled her eyes but the smile on her face said exactly what I needed to hear.

# Chapter Eight

*Vivi*

I thought spending the day in bed with Jag's body as my playground would have made me relaxed and calm. I was wrong. After a few hours of deep, dreamless sleep I woke up around six in the morning with sore limbs and one little thought niggling over and over in my brain.

My contact. Bob. Bob had contacted me again about six months ago to decrypt the external hard drive but hadn't been in touch since. None of my calls were returned, not even the threatening ones. But this morning, for some fucking reason, I got it in my head to find out what the fuck was going on. So I called Bob again. Three times.

Bob didn't answer. Instead of leaving more irate messages, I grabbed my keys and my I.D. because I needed some fresh air. Some distance from Jag and all the thoughts racing through my mind. I needed my bike, dammit.

It took nearly an hour to get to the storage facility by bus where I hid my bike because apparently Las Vegas traffic was as bad as New York. The moment my two wheels hit the pavement though, everything else disappeared. No one was chasing me with plans to do who the fuck knew what with me. There were no distractions from my work and my adventures, and especially no tall, dark and deadly hot hacker with a military background. None of it mattered as I wove through traffic in an attempt to get on the freeway in this sea of streets that all led back to the cluster of casinos. The city's bread and butter was not what I wanted or needed right now.

Nope, I needed a long stretch of road where I could rev the engine and focus on nothing but the blur of the passing road. Riding was my favorite thing to do when I wasn't locked in my house working. And I rode for hours with the sun steadily rising at my back, I rode until all the thoughts and worries...all the fucking noise disappeared and left nothing but the facts.

Suddenly my mind went back about seven years ago when I'd taken a few college classes for shits and giggles. And to prove I could, of course.

I took a journalism class and the professor, whose name I couldn't remember, said something that came back to me when my mind was decluttered. Figuring out every story means figuring out the six major questions: Who, what, where, when, how and why. I already knew who—or I thought I did—and I knew what. Basically. But I needed to know why it was such a problem that I'd seen what I saw. If I could figure that out, I could beat this fucker at his own game.

Assuming said fucker was Governor Blaise and not the gangster who looked like he'd smack his own mother if there was some benefit to it. Otherwise, I was totally fucked.

My back started to ache from riding too long, so I stopped at a greasy spoon diner for a bowl of chili and got back on the road, energized to figure this shit out.

Optimism was totally out of character for me and that should have been a clue that something was about to spoil my almost good mood.

I'd spotted a shiny red pickup truck on my ass ever since I'd left the diner and he was following too damn close. Not that anyone with a ride that flashy could ever be accused of being subtle, but he was doing a piss poor job of remaining unseen, which meant I needed to put some distance between us. I gunned the engine and split between a big rig and a minivan, speeding ten cars ahead. But this time of day, the traffic was light, and the big red asshole was gaining on me.

I slowed down, staying between the right and middle lanes and switching it up whenever he got too close. And when he was right on my ass, I sped up and flew around a curve hoping that I would lose him but once again the universe conspired against me and he was right there. My speedometer needle jerked past ninety miles and it continued to climb but there was a curve up ahead and I needed to slow down.

# HEAVENLY HACKED

But I couldn't. He was gaining on me but speeding up was certain death where this asshole was...*un*certain. "Shit!" The impact was brief and jarring, and just enough to make my bike tire stop and then spin until the whole bike was out of control and careening down a ravine. It was no more than twenty or thirty feet but even with my leathers on it hurt like a motherfucker. Especially when my helmet was kindly stopped by a giant rock.

The only thing I could think of as I lay there trying to catch my breath was that I fucking hurt and I wasn't going to die out here.

I held my breath for ninety seconds when a car came to a stop above. I assumed it was the red truck douchebag making sure he scared or killed me. I stayed as still as I could, waiting for the sound of footsteps on the dry grass and graveled path I just skidded down. But they never came. At the seventieth second the door slammed shut and the engine gunned but still, I waited until the ninety second mark. "Fuck."

My chest heaved, and I focused on my legs first, to see if I felt any broken bones. My toes wiggled, and I exhaled. Thank the Man above. Both of my arms were intact, so I slowly slid off my helmet and got up on my knees and looked around. "Fuck!"

I searched for my phone that had flown from my pocket and saw it about ten feet away. I rolled over to my phone, afraid to get up. My body could go into shock any minute and I had to get a hold of Jag before that happened.

My hands shook so bad it took nearly a minute just to get the fingerprint unlock on my phone to work. When it opened I took a deep breath and squeezed my eyes shut until I saw stars. I needed to concentrate. To focus. There were no details to recall other than the flashy red pickup with the extended cab. I spoke the details into the notepad app when a thought occurred to me and I slid back over to my bike. There was no way in hell those guys had found me by accident.

I searched behind the tail light, the fender and even the goddamn safety bar before I found what I was looking for. A tracker. It was no bigger than a SIM card and wasn't even pro or military grade. Cheap fuckers. I shoved it in my pocket and called Jag.

"Since your camper is still here I assume you didn't run?"

He was such a ballbuster. "You know what happens when you assume, Jeremiah." A groan came out when I tried to stand and I was starting to think maybe I was more banged up than I realized. "Do you know the name of a tow company?"

He was quiet for a second, probably trying to figure me out. Good luck. I'd been trying to figure that shit out all my life. "Gunnar has a towing company in town. He can take care of you."

"No. I don't want a company associated with your club." I realized how that sounded after I said it. "I didn't mean it like that, just give me the name of another? Please?"

"Fine. Where are you?"

"I don't even know. I'll text you from my GPS app."

"Okay, I'll be right there."

He hung up and I texted my GPS location to him. I fell back on the ground and rolled my eyes, laughing on the inside at the absurdity of my life now. Chasing down a man I'd never met but crushed on and dodging a possible government conspiracy out to kill me for a few photos. It sounded batshit crazy to me and I was living it. Or I was in the matrix, which could be kind of cool since it would mean none of this was real, but that would mean last night with Jeremiah wasn't real either.

Damn. My head hurt. Was I dreaming?

The sound of a motorcycle engine grew closer and stopped and I knew it was Jag. Then he spoke and confirmed my suspicions. "What in the hell happened? I'll call the ambulance."

## HEAVENLY HACKED

"No! You can't!" I looked up at a very worried and very ruggedly handsome face. "How'd you get here so fast?"

"Shit," he grumbled and with impressive speed jogged down the ravine and knelt down beside me. "Are you okay? Fuck, Vivi. Talk to me. Did you hit your head?" His hands felt nice even though his touch was medical not intimate.

"I'm talking. I had my helmet on. I'm okay, just banged up." His big strong hands were warm against my skin, roaming to check my head, my neck, my ribs. "Quit trying to cop a feel."

His lips smirked at me, but his eyes glared. "I'm just making sure you don't have any broken bones."

"I don't." I smacked his hands away because they felt too good and because when Jag was being all sweet and concerned and shit, he reminded me of the boy I loved until he left me. "Did you call the tow truck?"

"I did but your bike is thrashed."

Typical guy. "Yeah, I know." He gave me an odd look, probably expecting an explanation but I just stared at him. To be stubborn sure, but he was nice to look at. Very nice.

"Let me help you," he said. But instead of waiting for me to agree, he scooped me in his arms like I weighed nothing, and I weighed a lot more than nothing. I was five-seven with more ass and tits than I needed, so again, I weighed a lot more than nothing. But the way he carried me up the ravine without breaking a sweat or heaving for air turned me on. Or maybe it was just him. Jag. He smelled like a man. A real man who got his hands dirty and had dirt streaked on his face.

"You smell good."

He smirked. "You definitely hit your head if you're giving me a compliment."

I frowned. "I said you were beautiful."

Jag let out a snort. "Only because you wanted my dick."

## HEAVENLY HACKED

That made me grin. "It worked. But you are. Beautiful, I mean." Shit, I did hit my head. And it hurt like a mother fucker.

By the time we got to the road the tow truck had arrived.

"You can ride with me," he said. He led me to his bike and set me down on a nearby boulder before going to talk to the tow truck guy like I was some little lady who needed to be handled.

"Don't try to manage me, Jeremiah!" He didn't respond, and I sat there for what felt like forever and then finally, we were moving. "I could have taken care of that myself."

"You're welcome, Vivi," he called over his shoulder. "Stubborn ass woman."

Stubborn was a word I'd heard a lot, but most people weren't as polite as Jag and preferred the word bitch. "I'll be right back," I told him when we got to the towing company.

"I don't think so." He grabbed my arm. "You may be capable and stubborn and probably deadly, but right now you may be in shock and also have a concussion. I'll stay close."

"But I'll—"

"Handle it," he finished with a patient smile. "Got it."

Ugh, why did he have to be devilishly hot but sweet as pie? I couldn't let those girlhood dreams bubble up just because he was being nice. I still didn't know the new Jag. "Good."

At the counter, the guy who'd towed my bike leaned close trying to get a good look at my tits. I didn't care, as long as he didn't touch. "Not much I can do tonight but write up a ticket for the tow."

I nodded and stuck my chest out a little more. "That's fine, it's just … do you have any loaner cars here?" His gaze slid down and then with some effort, back up to my face.

## HEAVENLY HACKED

"We do but we only issue 'em between eight and seven." The guy, Dennis his coveralls said, seemed genuinely beat up about it. Probably hoping I'd blow him to get an eighties Corvette or something. "But you can look around a minute and if you find one you like I'll make sure they hold it for ya."

"Really?" I leaned forward with a grateful smile as he nodded, his gaze no longer even pretending my face held any interest. "Thank you so much, Dennis. I'll be right back okay?" He nodded, licking his lips and probably doing God only knows what to me in his mind.

"Yeah, sure thing sweetheart."

I rolled my eyes because old guys like that just couldn't help themselves. He could jerk off in the shower to my tits while his wife read the latest tie-me-up-and-fuck-me-hard romance novels in the bedroom. It was the least I could do for the institution of marriage.

The loaner lot wasn't all that big with maybe twenty cars. Most were mid to high range sedans that probably belonged to people with families. And then I saw it, there in the back, the perfect car. An older model Crown Vic, desperately in need of service but still active. It would throw them off my scent and maybe land them in a fuck ton of trouble.

"You could have just told me what you were up to." Jag's voice was right behind me and when I stood my ass brushed against him.

"Don't sneak up on me!" I turned to face him and knelt down, never taking my eyes off Jag as I placed the tracker just above the rear tire.

"I didn't sneak, I walked." He stood closer, his denim covered cock just inches from my mouth. My watering mouth. "Come on, spy girl." He held his hand out and I took it, ignoring the sizzle snaking from my palm to his.

"That's spy woman to you."

He smiled but there was something else on his mind. "You could have just told me your plan."

## HEAVENLY HACKED

"And have you try to talk me out of it? It was easier this way."

"For you, maybe."

"Yeah well, I'm the one who was run off the road by a big red monster truck."

His expression changed, and he stayed quiet as I said an enthusiastic goodbye to Dennis and left to get on his bike.

"You could have been killed."

"Duh, I think that was kind of the point."

"You think you're ok to ride? Not going to hurt too much? I can get us a car."

I threw my leg cautiously over the bike and sat down. "I'm fine. Let's just go home."

Jag stayed silent for the entire ride back to his place, which was a long ride, because it wasn't on the Vegas side of Mayhem. He killed the engine and stepped off his bike silently, holding my hand with a gentle kind of intensity I didn't know how to take. Not with my head so fuzzy and my body so achy.

We walked up to the front door and slowly went inside.

Jag undressed me, giving me a moment to look around the room while he went to start the water in the tub. I'd spent hours in this room, too distracted with his naked body to take in the dark, masculine details. The room was two shades of green with cherry furniture. Stylish but not fussy, exactly like the man who occupied it.

"Come on." He took my hand and pulled me into the bathroom where the tub was almost full with steaming, scented water. "Get in. It'll help with your pain."

I wanted to, but my senses were tingling, telling me to proceed with caution. "What's the catch?"

He rolled his eyes and pushed me toward the tub, tapping one leg to get me to lift it. "I can lift you and put you in if you'd prefer."

## HEAVENLY HACKED

I would prefer dammit, but not now. I stepped in and sank into the water with a moan. It was perfectly hot and smelled faintly of Jag. "Are you going to join me?"

"Not yet. First I want you to tell me what you haven't told me yet."

And there it was.

The trap.

# Chapter Nine

*Jag*

This was the first time since I became a Reckless Bastard that the club didn't have my full attention. I couldn't stop thinking about the fact that someone had run Vivi off the fucking road. Still, Cross was talking and he was my Prez. I needed to fucking listen.

"Stitch has been on ID duty at one of the dispensaries and he's spotted a couple guys who look like feds hanging around. Anyone have any idea why?" Cross's blue gaze looked around the table, assessing each of us to see why the club might face another threat. His gaze landed on me, a question burning in the depths.

"This shit can't be placed at my door." That was serious. Of all the Reckless Bastards I was the squeakiest fucking clean. I didn't fuck the Reckless Bitches and I didn't get serious about women, which meant my personal shit never touched the club. Until now. Maybe.

"So this has nothing to do with the blue haired babe who came looking for you the other night?"

I couldn't definitively say it had nothing to do with Vivi, but I was pretty sure. "Probably not. Stitch. When did these suits first start showing up?"

"About a month ago, maybe six weeks. They've been around more in the last two weeks, though." Which meant well before Vivi reentered my life.

"Yeah, Vivi came because she needs my help but it's sensitive. Highly sensitive, Cross. I'm not keeping secrets." Cross nodded his acceptance, for now. But I wasn't foolish enough to think he'd stay that way forever.

"Fuck that," Savior spat out. "Just cut the shit and tell us what kind of trouble your girl is about to bring to our fucking door."

I glared at his fucking tone. "First of all, she's not my girl. She's a friend. Second, are we really about to pretend that half the guys at this table didn't have a woman bringing trouble in some form or another to our fucking door?" My gaze started with Savior, who had some nerve since he'd been involved in a fucking shootout in the middle of a casino, but Max, Golden Boy and Lasso all got looks from me as well.

"Not your girl? Then why the fuck are we even discussing this?" Savior spat out angrily. Again. He really needed to chill.

"Was Mandy your old lady when she came here? And wasn't it her who started this shit with Roadkill in the first place?" It was a low blow and I didn't blame her, but Savior's attitude was pissing me off.

"That's enough, Jag," Savior protested.

"Is it?" I stood, daring him to get in my face. Savior was crazy but I was a skilled fucking killer with more than a little crazy of my own.

"Stop!" Cross's voice cut through the macho bullshit, eyes blazing at us both. "What can you tell us?"

"She saw something she probably shouldn't have when she did some contract work for Uncle Sam and now she thinks someone with juice is after her." And after yesterday even I couldn't dismiss her concerns.

"Thinks?" Gunnar guffaws. "Tell this chick to hit the road. The last thing we need is any government bullshit blowing back on us." My hands balled into fists at his words but I gave Gunnar a break because I knew he had a lot of shit on his plate with a one-year old sister now in his care. Visits from a social worker were stressing him out so I let it go. For now.

I glared at my friend though to let him know he was on dangerous ground. "Since someone ran her off the road yesterday and she found a tracker on her bike, I'd say it's a bit more than a fucking hunch at this point. The bike is fucking totaled." Just thinking about those assholes pissed me off and the way Vivi played it off like it was no big deal pissed me off even more.

I hated that her life had been so hard that she felt so alone. But that was probably partially my fault too. Gunnar nodded, his eyes holding a hint of an apology.

## HEAVENLY HACKED

"Why didn't she bring the bike to me? Too good for a bunch of greasy bikers?"

"What the fuck is your problem?" Lasso snarled the question at him. "Don't be an asshole, Gunnar."

Gunnar shrugged, unapologetic.

"It's fine, Lasso," I told him. "She found a tracker like I said and instead of disabling it, she put it on an old police cruiser. She didn't want it traced back to the club if, by some chance, they made a connection between her and me." It was unlikely, but this was the U.S. government we were talking about. Shady as fuck.

"How exactly do you know her?" Golden Boy asked the question but there was no malice in it. "Because I've never heard you mention her."

I sighed and prepared myself for the bullshit that was about to ensue. "We met online as kids, became good friends and traded hacking tips. She was my best friend until Mom died."

They were all silent for several beats before the room erupted in laughter and jokes. "The only guy to really have a girlfriend in another town," Max guffawed.

"Aww, an online girlfriend!" Stitch grinned wide. "Did you guys do it in bits and bytes?"

"Very funny asshole." They kept it up for a few minutes and I let them because it was all in good fun and I really didn't care.

"All right. If we have no more actual business to discuss, this meeting is adjourned." We all stood and started to filter out of the room, but I stayed because I owed Cross more.

He looked up from his phone. "You have more to say?"

I nodded and closed the door, giving Cross a quick but vague rundown of the situation with the Governor. "She seems pretty sure it's this governor and given his political aspirations and the illegal aspect of his relationship, I'm inclined to agree. But I think there's another option she hasn't told me about."

He frowned. "Why? I thought you were friends."

"We are. But I lost my shit after my mom died and cut myself off from everyone, even Vivi. But I do know her and she's a terrible fucking liar. She's afraid and not sure if she can trust us—or me—but she will."

Cross nodded. "How is she doing?"

"Stubborn as hell," I told him with a smile, thinking about my terrible little patient. "Bruised and banged up and mad as hell about it. She's ready to destroy everyone involved."

Cross laughed. "You're gonna have your hands full."

"Looks like." And honestly, I had no worried worries about it. I could handle Vivi just fine.

"So that's it, huh? She's the kind of girl who grabs your attention?"

It was true that I didn't pay much attention to women unless I was in the mood to fuck. I didn't do relationships, so I understood his surprise. "Believe it or not, I never knew what she looked like until she showed up here. She wouldn't meet me back when we were kids."

"That's not what I mean. I always thought you'd go for the sweet, docile type. Like a schoolteacher or something but Vivi looks a touch tough and badass. Like way more woman than I thought you'd ever want."

"You saw those legs, right?" His grin matched my own as I thought about those long legs wrapped around me while I fucked her all over my bedroom. That was two days ago. Too fucking long.

"I'll see what else I can find out. With her help I'll find out what the fuck is up with those Feds and Roadkill too."

Cross looked shocked by my words but he only nodded. "Good. Keep me in the loop and I'll have a chat with Savior."

"Don't bother." I didn't give a shit. Not with Vivi waiting at home for me. "Later."

## Chapter Ten

*Vivi*

Another day had come and gone holed up at Jag's and still no fucking word from Bob. I was officially beyond pissed off and secretly hoping that the reason she hadn't called back yet was because she couldn't. Permanently couldn't. Not that I wanted any harm to come to Bob, I just wanted to come up with a reason for her radio silence. On top of all that, I couldn't even peek inside my apartment since all the cameras had been removed. By the damn police who wouldn't stop calling me.

After two days of nonstop calls, I picked up angrily. "Yes, Detective, I am very much alive and well and I'd like to stay that way."

"Do you have any idea who could be behind this, Ms. Montgomery?"

Not any answer he would believe. "Not a clue, so if you could find out who the fuck ran me off the road, I'll donate a thousand bucks to the Police Foundation." That came dangerously close to bribing an official, but desperate times called for desperate measures.

The detective sighed. "Ma'am we can't keep you safe if we don't know where you are."

"You can't keep me safe anyway, Detective. But I can keep me safe until you find this psycho. I promise to keep you updated regularly."

He waited a beat and when the detective spoke, there was resignation in his voice. "Fine. You can reach me at—"

"I'll have no problem finding you," I told him and ended the call quickly. The last thing I needed was someone else on Governor Blaise's payroll able to find me. Then again, with that tracker they knew I was in or near Vegas.

Done with one set of lawmen, I turned my attention to another duo, specifically the two federal agents from the photos. I already knew they were Agents Ryan and Hewitt and in less than an hour I had their home and cell phone numbers, personal and work email addresses and all kinds of other personal information that two members of law enforcement should know better than to make it so easy. Lucky for them, I just wanted information, not to ruin their lives.

Not yet, anyway.

Armed with things like wives' birthdays and anniversaries it took me no time at all to pull up phone records, which was where I struck gold. Or at least gold plated. Two phone numbers appeared too frequently to be a stranger but not nearly enough to be a mistress. And the most fucked up part of all? Both numbers had Nevada area codes and a quick reverse number search produced one result. Vigo Rizzoli, a name that meant nothing at all to me but gave me another string to start pulling. "Got it!" The other number belonged to Roadkill MC, a motorcycle club located in the heart of Las Vegas.

That definitely was not a fucking coincidence, and further digging showed that Vigo Rizzoli wasn't just a member of the club, he was the goddamn VP. Those familiar tingles that had helped me avoid real danger my whole life, began at my toes and quickly worked their way up. A picture was forming in my mind, but I couldn't see all of it. But the deeper I dug into Roadkill, the more shit I found I didn't want to know—coke, heroin, underage girls, guns and even contract killings. And the more I found out, the more I began to think that coming to Vegas—to Jag—might have been my biggest mistake of all.

The online police blotters for both Mayhem and Las Vegas proper revealed a longstanding feud between Roadkill and the Reckless Bastards, with group arrests going back years and years. I didn't know what it meant, yet, but I would.

I hoped.

Doubts began to creep in and I couldn't stop them. Doubts about whether or not I could trust Jag. He was in a club. They were also a club. What if both clubs did business together and giving him this bit of information only put me in more trouble? I trusted Jag, or at least I thought I did. For now I would keep it to myself.

"Hey. How are you feeling?"

Jag's voice startled me and pulled me from my thoughts. I slammed my laptop shut and looked at him with a blank expression. "Fine. It's not like I'm a delicate flower or anything."

He rolled his eyes but the smile that pulled his lush lips up at the corner made my pussy clench. Damn stupid lady hormones. "Good. Let's go."

"Where?" I stayed where I was with my arms crossed, waiting for more details.

"Just come on. And grab your helmet." Damn stubborn man just walked off but not before I saw the smirk on his face. He was enjoying bossing me around.

"You're lucky you look good walking away or else I would've thrown something at your head." His laughter sounded but he didn't respond. I didn't mind;

he had a really nice ass. "My bike is totaled," I reminded him when we got to the garage.

His mouth pulled to one side in a smirk. "Then I guess you better hold on tight." I should have tossed my helmet at him but the sight of Jag, all big and strong as he started the motorcycle engine, had my body responding and suddenly I couldn't wait to wrap my arms around him.

I held on tight as he let the engine roar, zooming down the road and weaving through traffic. When he soared around the curves, dipping low to one side, I held on even tighter. His body was hard and his male potency combined with the engine between my thighs, had my pussy pulsing and my nipples tingling beneath my leather jacket. We stopped in a strip mall parking lot and I slid off, feeling that familiar sensation as my legs readjusted to solid ground again. "What are we doing here?"

He pointed to a sign over a shop that said Green Mayhem. "Gotta fix some computer shit real quick."

# HEAVENLY HACKED

"Real quick for real?" He smiled and nodded before disappearing inside, leaving me alone and leaning against the wall while I stared at the bike. I looked around at the dispensary and it looked just like what I'd seen in Colorado and Washington, in a long row of other businesses that sold everything from power tools to prom dresses, yarn and sneakers.

But across the street my gaze drifted over something that gave me pause. A big ass, look-at-me bright red extended cab pickup. Nevada had a lot of fucking trucks, probably more red ones than any other color but I couldn't take my eyes off it. Something told me I should get closer, get the plate so I could run it later, and my feet were already moving in that direction. If I could just get close enough.

"You should watch the company you keep." I didn't recognize the voice, clearly male and angry for some reason. I looked to my right to find a skinny asshole with long blond hair standing about five feet away from me.

Too damn close for my comfort. "And you should mind your own fucking business." I slid one hand down my hip and around to my back pocket and looped my thumb through the hook. A smile crossed my face as it always did when I got an opportunity to use my knife knuckles.

He took a step forward, his face marred with a dark anger I'd seen before. Men who didn't like mouthy women. "And you better watch how you speak to me, bitch." He got in my face and gave me exactly what I was looking for.

A chance to go crazy. The blade was out of my pocket in half a second with my fingers pushed through the holes, the cool metal of the knife pressed against his skin. I had at least two inches on him and pressed my knee between his legs, daring him to move. "You were saying, limp dick?"

His eyes, green I realized, went wide. Big as saucers as they stared into my smiling face.

"You're crazy."

## HEAVENLY HACKED

"Oh, you have no fucking idea how crazy," I told him with a wild laugh. "But let's talk about you, Limp Dick. Who the fuck do you think you are, telling me who I should spend my time with? What business is it of yours?"

"I-it's not. Get off me you crazy bitch!" He let out a gurgle when I applied just a bit more pressure that made me laugh.

"You really ought to watch that mouth of yours. Show a little respect before someone washes your mouth out with soap." I was having too much fun with this clown. "Better yet, maybe someone ought to cut out your tongue."

"Vivi, what the fuck?" Jag. Here to ruin my fun.

"Crazy bitch," the blond said again and shoved me since I was distracted. Not too distracted to land a blow to his right cheek that sent him to his knees.

"Next time I'll bring soap." I laughed as he scrambled away, looking at me like I'd lost my mind.

"Keep your bitch in check, Jag!"

"Fuck off, Carter, before I let her have her way with you." Jag's face was twisted in an anger I'd never seen before, even as he was trying to push me behind him. Protective jerk.

"Watch yourself, bitch."

I laughed. "Go home and change your shitty drawers, pussy!" Another laugh bubbled up out of me at the absurdness of the past five minutes until I was doubled over and tearing up from laughter.

Jag bent down so we were face to face, one brow arched in a *what the fuck* expression. "Can't take you anywhere."

"Apparently not. That was fun, though."

"He might be right. You are crazy."

"Just a teensy bit," I told him, thumb and forefinger just a few millimeters apart.

He flashed another one of those panty incinerating smiles and hooked an arm around my waist. "Come on, Bruiser. We have an appointment to keep."

## HEAVENLY HACKED

"We do?" The irritating man stayed silent on the way to wherever we were going, not uttering one word until he came to a stop in front of a very nice two-story family home in a gated subdivision.

"Here we are."

"This is our appointment?" I pointed at the suburban monstrosity.

"Yes. Come on." He pulled me inside of a furnished but unlived in home. "This is the quick dime tour."

I laughed as my gaze bounced off what few details there were—basic farmhouse-style furniture in soothing shades of blue and green, plain pale blue walls and an exposed beam kitchen—while Jag pulled me through to the backyard. "That tour was worth way less than a dime. I expect some change back."

"I'm fresh out of cash. I'll get you later," he said, flashing that slow burning smile that did things to my insides. "Let's have a seat." He curled his body around me on a large lounger in the center of the yard, overlooking an egg-shaped pool.

"This place is nice. Yours or the club's?"

"Mine. This house is the dream of a future I'm not sure I'll have. But if I do…" he said but never finished.

"You'll already have the house?"

"Yeah, something like that." He pulled a joint from his pocket and sparked it, taking a long pull before handing it to me.

"I haven't smoked pot since I was twenty-one. You know the feds drug test." And it was damn good quality. I took three more hits until I felt weightless in his arms. Until all I could feel was his warm skin and the only thing I could smell was his clean, masculine scent. I let my body revel in being this close to him. I rarely allowed this level of closeness with anyone but right now, I let myself enjoy it.

"I know you're not telling me everything, Vivi."

So much for enjoyment. "And?"

"And I don't like it. But dammit, Vivi, I couldn't stand it if something happened to you."

I nodded at his words and stood, feeling uncomfortable with the emotion I heard in his voice. There weren't any people left in my life who cared. There were people I knew, people who I was useful to or were useful to me. A few might be considered friends, but the rest were acquaintances at best. Colleagues, really.

So I buried down the soft, vulnerable feelings that threatened to rise up and I stripped right in front of him before slipping into the pool. I swam the length and back, clearing my mind and berating myself for wanting to tell him everything. I would, but not yet. "What the—" I spluttered as my forward movement was halted by a hand wrapped around my ankle.

"You are fucking stubborn as hell, woman." He tugged me closer until our naked bodies were lined up perfectly.

"Hey." My voice was breathless, projecting just how turned on I was by this man.

"Hey back." His lips pulled into a smile and then his mouth was attacking mine in a frenzy of raw hunger. It was a kiss unlike any I'd ever felt before, hitting me right between the legs and I wrapped myself around him. I needed to get closer. I had to. But before I could, he lifted me out of the water and onto the cool concrete, with my legs spread wide he buried his face between my legs and did the thing he did so well.

I looked up at the darkening sky while Jag ate my pussy and brought me to sexual heights I'd never experienced. And when my orgasm came on violently, he didn't even give me a chance to come down before I was back in the water and sliding down his cock. "Oh fuck!"

He didn't let up, driving deep and hard into me, the water making it feel like we were floating in the air.

"Vivi. So perfect. So fucking tight."

His deep growling voice was adding more fuel to the fire and my hips began to swirl and pump against him.

# HEAVENLY HACKED

"Jag, please. More."

"Vivi," he growled again, sliding us over until his feet were on the bottom of the pool. Then he fucked me like his life depended on it, hard and fast and so damn deep I was pretty sure he couldn't get any deeper.

"Oh fuck," I moaned, gripping him tighter as he pumped harder and deeper. And then I was swimming in the most overwhelming orgasm of my life. Maybe it was the pot, but it was probably the man. The man still thrusting into me as pleasure kept me in a hazy fog that stole my breath and made me dizzy. "Damn."

His smile was intense as he kept thrusting until a low growl escaped and those last few strokes pulled a second orgasm out of me just as his own orgasm vibrated through both of us, causing small waves in the pool. "Fuck, Vivi. You undo me."

"Ditto, Jeremiah." His breaths were fast and shallow, matching mine as we stared at each other in wonder. That passion, that intensity had come out of nowhere. Burning hot and fast.

That was probably a fitting foreshadowing of how things were destined to end.

# Chapter Eleven

*Jag*

"What the hell do you think you're doing?" I'd spotted Vivi across the street from GET INK'D at the end of my afternoon shift and she was taking pictures. Lasso and I swung wide to cross the street without her noticing.

Vivi gasped and whirled on me, fingers pushed the brass knuckles with the knife aimed in my direction. "Goddammit Jeremiah, don't sneak up on me!"

Lasso stepped forward and I waved him off, grabbing her wrist so the blade was pointed at the ground. "You have an unhealthy affinity for that knife, babe."

"It's not unhealthy. This knife has never failed me. Ever." Her expression was cool and serious. I wondered what had happened to her when I dropped off the face of the planet. "And it helps when people think it's a good idea to sneak up on others."

She was right about that, especially a woman as conspicuous as she was. "What did that redneck wagon do to piss you off?"

Once I crossed the street it was easy to tell, if I looked close enough, that for her attempts to look like a casual photographer, she was definitely focused on the red pickup.

"I don't know what you're talking about." She tucked the knife into her back pocket and crossed her arms, scanning the landscape but her eyes never strayed too long from the red truck.

"Come on, sweetheart. You're good but you're not that good," Lasso told her. "You're clocking that truck. Wanna tell us why?"

She turned gray eyes on Lasso. "No. Now if you don't mind...fuck!" She turned, and her shoulders fell as the red truck pulled into traffic and turned at the first visible light. "Thanks boys, you've been a big fucking help." Vivi slapped the cap on the lens of the expensive camera that hung from her neck and shoulder checked me as she passed and ran into Lasso.

# HEAVENLY HACKED

"Whoa there, sweetheart. Shit...I said whoa, goddammit!" Lasso's blue eyes went wide when Vivi tried to punch him. "I'm just trying to steady you woman. Damn!"

"That's my friend and fellow Reckless Bastard, Lasso."

She rolled her eyes and took a step away from Lasso and then another. "Do any of you have normal names?"

"Says the chick named Vivi," Lasso snickered.

"Short for Genevieve. Is yours short for Lasso's A Lotta Pussy?" I never would have believed there was anything on God's green earth that would make Lasso blush. Until now.

A laugh burst out of me and for a minute I couldn't control myself. "That's pretty close, actually." Lasso glared at me but Vivi, she just looked...uninterested, but I knew that wasn't it, which meant she was biding her time.

"You saw more than what you let on," I accused.

"No. I saw a big flashy ass red truck and I used the brains in my head to make a few deductions. The only reason to use an obnoxious vehicle like that to do surveillance is because it's yours, which pegged him as a local."

She gave me a look that said I should have figured all that out on my own and she wasn't wrong.

"And now I've wasted a day with no fucking answers so I'm going to get some food." Her legs were on the move again but I kept up with her.

"Sounds good. Where are we going?"

"We aren't going anywhere. I prefer to eat alone."

I smiled at her petulance. "I prefer to eat with company, especially when I can't eat the company. Yet." She skipped a step but I didn't call her on it.

"I didn't need to hear that," Lasso said, sounding disgruntled. "Unless you want to give me more details."

"He doesn't," Vivi shot at Lasso, glaring over her shoulder.

## HEAVENLY HACKED

"It was worth an ask." Without looking I could hear the smile in Lasso's voice. "Anyway Rocky is making enchiladas tonight. They're my favorite."

"Sounds good to me." I grabbed Vivi's hand and tugged her in the direction of my bike. "Come on. We'll meet you there, man."

Vivi of course never did anything easily and yanked out of my grasp. "You boys have fun." She turned but I had her wrist before she moved two steps. "Get your hands off me."

"No. Settle the fuck down. I'll help you ID the driver of the red truck. Right now, though, I really fucking want some of those enchiladas."

Those gray eyes looked so deep into me that I was pretty sure they saw straight through me, down to the parts of me I hid from everyone. Even myself.

"You are completely ridiculous, I hope you know that," she said and pushed me away, but instead of walking away she went and grabbed my helmet off my bike and slid it on, taking the driver's position. "Hop on."

"I don't think so, babe." My hand cupped her thigh as she lifted herself up to kickstart the engine. "My ride. I drive."

She rolled her eyes and straightened her leather jacket. "You want me to go to dinner at some stranger's house then you get on and hang on."

"Since you make it sound so appealing," I told her with a laugh and pulled the extra helmet from the storage kit, snapping it under my chin like a teenager. When I stepped over the bike and put my hands on Vivi, holding her slender waist as the bike vibrated underneath us, I wondered why in the hell I ever resisted in the first place. She shivered when my thumb scraped across that strip of skin at her midriff and I smiled. I got hard just thinking about bringing a tough chick like Vivi to her knees.

She was a seasoned rider, I could tell by the way she rode effortlessly. Vivi didn't get spooked when she was cut off or by chronic brakers. She leaned easily into the turns, speeding up and weaving through Sunday drivers without hesitation. She pulled into the driveway beside Lasso and pulled off the helmet.

"You'll pay for that later," she snarled at me.

"I'm counting on it, tough girl." She glared at me and then she growled, and my cock grew hard behind my zipper.

She rolled her eyes again, her default when she was uncomfortable I was starting to learn. "I don't really feel like hanging out with your friends, Jag."

"They're not just my friends. They're my family. Even if you don't give a damn about them, you have to eat." I knew she'd argue because like I said, Vivi didn't do anything easy. So I cut her off before she could form an argument, pulling her close and taking her mouth like I wanted to since I spotted her behind the camera. Her lips were soft and tasted like cherries, deepening my need to devour her sweet mouth. When she succumbed to me I wished we were anywhere else so I could lay her out and make her come until she was totally undone.

Her hands fisted at my waistband and I knew one of us had to pull back and it had to be me. "You seem like a nice guy," she panted with a wild-eyed smile, "but you fight dirty." With a shake of her head, Vivi pushed at my chest again and followed Lasso inside.

\*\*\*

I woke up with a heavy blue silk curtain covering my face. Moonlight sliced through the window, highlighting her pale skin and the stark contrasts between us. My hand on her thigh was near black and I couldn't look away from the beauty of it. I turned, ready to wake her up and take her again because apparently, I couldn't get enough of sexy, foul-mouthed Vivi. And then my phone vibrated on the nightstand.

I reached out blindly for the phone and groaned at the name. Slauson. It was a call I'd been waiting for and not even Vivi could distract me. I stepped into my boxers and took my phone into the living room. "Slauson, what the fuck?"

"I need your help," she said, sounding more worried than I'd ever heard Slauson sound. "I have an asset in trouble and she's been out of contact for more than forty-eight hours. Well, probably longer but things are kind of fucked up here right now."

Immediately I was on edge. The hairs on my body stood up, electrified like some magnet vortex had been created in my living room.

"Give me a name."

I had a feeling I knew the name. That the asset she was missing was asleep in my bed even though I had nothing more than a hunch. A gut reaction. "I can't help them if I don't know who they are, Slauson."

"I know," she sighed. Her voice trembled, and I could hear just how distraught she was. "This is all just so fucked. I don't know how…" She let out another long breath.

"Just tell me." I tried to keep a leash on my temper because I recognized that if Slauson was worried, we should all be worried.

There was a long pause that tested the fuck out of my temper but finally she spoke. "There's a leak and I haven't figured out who yet. Her name is Genie. Find Genie and I'll be in touch."

"How in the hell am I supposed find someone based on that?" The line was silent but there was still sound. "Slauson? Goddammit, Slauson!" The timer on the call continued to climb but there was no sound. No struggle, no gunshot, nothing. Just pure fucking quiet. "Slauson!"

"Why are you talking to Bob?" Vivi's voice was icy cold and filled with accusation.

I turned with a scowl. "Who the fuck is Bob?"

"Bob Slauson, the person you were just swearing at into the phone. The same person I've been trying to reach for days who, conveniently, has been out of

# HEAVENLY HACKED

touch. And now she's calling you in the middle of the night. Why?"

This conversation had the potential to go sideways quick and I didn't have the energy for this shit. But one of us needed to be calm and Vivi was all fired up.

I shrugged. "I still do contract work for the government." Her eyes widened and she stepped back. "Dammit, Vivi not that kind of contract work. Logistics and finding people. Basic cyber security shit." It was the honest truth but the way she stepped back, wide gray eyes nearly silver said she didn't like my answer.

"You should have said something," she accused again, pulling my t-shirt over her head as she walked back into the bedroom. I wasn't foolish enough to think Vivi getting naked meant I was about to get my dick wet, and that thought was confirmed when she began to search my dark bedroom for her clothes.

"They're out in the living room," I told her and stepped back so she could get them, and she did, but not before grabbing her phone and purse. "What's the big damn deal?"

"The big damn deal," she said as she shoved her legs into her jeans, "is that you want me to trust you, yet you keep lying to me. For all I know, Bob just told you to put two bullets in my head."

I clamped my jaws together and clenched my fists at her words. I would never put my hands on a woman but dammit she pissed me off.

"You're not fucking funny."

"I'm not trying to be! But I think I'm going to sleep in my camper tonight."

"Take the spare room."

She glared at me. "No thanks." Vivi yanked her shirt over her head and tucked her shoes under her arm before storming out. Even though she was mad as hell at me, all I could think about was how beautiful she looked when she got all pissy.

I could see Vivi's point and how this all looked, but it was nothing like that and tomorrow over breakfast I would make her see that. I couldn't sleep for shit, wondering how in the hell I went from being wrapped around a gorgeous woman to alone in the same bed in the span of an hour.

She'd been so damn snarky lately, but there were these moments when I got a glimpse of the girl she used to be. A certain word said with a smile and I could remember a thousand conversations when I'd heard that smile. I hated to think what events had conspired to make her so mistrustful and jumpy, but every day I spent with her made me wonder. Eventually, I fell asleep with the scent of Vivi all around me. I'd clear up the misunderstanding in the morning.

After I'd slept for a few hours, I made a pot of coffee and went to the camper to apologize but it was locked. Even the windows and the top emergency hatch were locked up tight and through the slivers between the blinds I saw no signs of life.

Vivi was gone.

# KB WINTERS

## Chapter Twelve

*Vivi*

I used to think people who drove around in Priuses were pretentious assholes, and then I rode in a Tesla and I loved it so much I'd been thinking about moving out of the city to someplace where I could actually drive a car to the market or the movie theater.

When the bored kid with the Bieber haircut behind the counter at the car rental agency offered it up, I balked at first. But on day two of spying on Roadkill MC I could appreciate the silence of the engine and the plain blue color that meant the world that worshipped luxury vehicles and alpha dog motorcycles would look right past me. And that allowed me to get up close. Really close.

I'd worked out the hierarchy based on photos, and maybe there was a little bit of cell phone hackery, but not much. I just wanted to hear what they were talking about, like if they were in search of a blue-haired woman with a hit on her. I hadn't heard anything like that, but I'd gotten a few names of the guys in charge because they ran their shit like a combination between a board of trustees and military chain of command. It was damn confusing and on top of all that, no one had normal fucking names.

I was close to the converted artist's loft building that belonged to the Roadkill MC because I wanted to get a look inside. Since I wasn't dumb enough to try and walk right in, I decided to hack their security feed. It was pitiful, really. Then again, maybe not all biker gangs had a tech expert like Jag on their payroll.

There were plenty of women in short skirts and tight pants, every single one of their belly buttons on display. Nearly all of them seemed to be in their twenties—maybe early thirties—but every single one of them looked...*haggard*. Everyone had a drink in hand, some guys also had a girl or two in hand while others played pool or cards. It was just after noon and the party was in full swing.

Maybe the outlaw life wasn't so bad.

## HEAVENLY HACKED

When a black haired dude with a goatee shouted, "Hey Rizzoli," that got my attention because that name had been an earwig of the worst type. I held my breath and watched the screen, waiting for Rizzoli to enter the frame and hoping like hell it was the guy from the photo. It wasn't him, but this guy was clearly his brother. Maybe even his twin.

"What's up, man?" Other Rizzoli had a wide grin as he greeted everyone with an overeager hug and handshake.

"Where's Big Rizzoli?"

Other Rizzoli frowned but it only lasted a nanosecond. I knew they couldn't show emotions in this kind of toxic, excessively masculine, environment. It was actually quite sad. "He'll be here soon, said he had some business to take care of."

"Yeah, probably meeting with the Feds," I said to the screen, in the silent, air conditioned-comfort of my rental. I listened and made notes on everything I thought I might need to know about these guys. But mostly I was biding my time until the real Rizzoli showed up, the one from the pictures.

More than an hour had passed and the blonde wig I wore was starting to make me sweat even with the A/C on but finally the real Rizzoli appeared on the scene. Not in a red pickup truck but I didn't expect it to be quite that easy. I was hopeful but definitely not expectant. I snapped a few photos of the car, the plates and the man. Lots of close ups in hopes that maybe Peaches could work her magic. He didn't stay long, just long enough to take a duffel bag to a room in the back, drink a beer, grope a few girls and then he was gone.

There was a knock at my window and I jumped. I had a feeling I knew who it was, so I schooled my emotions and opened the window halfway. "Yes?"

Jag leaned down, forearms resting on the window's edge. "What are you doing here? And what's with the wig?"

"I'm doing recon. And Barbara has blonde hair." He smirked and then slid into the passenger seat.

"Why are you doing recon here?"

I shrugged, staring off in the distance because I still didn't know if the beef between Roadkill MC and Reckless Bastards was legitimate or for show. "Why not?"

"Come on, Vivi. You don't really think Slauson sent me to kill you, do you?"

No, I didn't. But Jag didn't need to know that. "I don't know, Jag. All I know is that I've been trying to get in touch with her and she hasn't called me back."

"And those two things equal me being a contract killer?" He was trying not to smile. I could hear it even though I wasn't looking at him.

"It means we don't tell each other everything and that's how it should stay."

"That's not good enough. Tell me why you're checking out Roadkill MC or I'll go in there and ask them." He was getting angry and even though my brain wanted to hurl insults at him, my nipples puckered and my clit swelled with desire. It was a real fucking conundrum.

"Because you're such good friends? Go ahead."

"So you can take off the minute I get out? I don't think so, babe."

"What are you doing here?" I was curious how he found me since I used an alias at the hotel and the car rental place, but I'd never ask. I knew he had the skills.

"You left in the middle of the night. Are you really that surprised?"

"My camper is at your place, Jag. I would have been back." Eventually. Probably in the middle of the night. Again. "Someone who owns a red truck is a known associate of a member of this club. Happy?" That was sort of true.

He sighed and rested a hand on top of mine. "I should have told you even though I haven't done any work for them in over six months. I called Slauson to see if she knew anything about your problem and the first I heard from her was that phone call."

## HEAVENLY HACKED

I held up a hand to stop him. "You know what? I shouldn't have come to you. Let's chalk it up to childish nostalgia."

"Bullshit." He bit the word out, hard and angry.

I sucked in a breath to give Jag a piece of my mind but a bullet pierced the windshield, whizzing between us and lodging in the backseat cupholder. "Shit." I turned over the engine but the damn thing was so silent, I forgot it was running. "What the fuck?"

"Drive! Keep your head down!"

I had at least enough presence of mind to stomp on the accelerator. The moves were instinctive, just a way to put some distance between us and the source of the bullets. "It's kind of hard to do both!" Driving with my head down kind of impeded my ability to see but with every stop sign I ignored, the sounds quieted until they stopped. "Holy fuck!"

"Did you see who was shooting at us?"

"Hell no but my guess is one of your Roadkill buddies."

"Oh that's right, find a way to blame me."

"If you hadn't distracted me then I would have been paying attention! Dammit!" I needed some time and some space to think. To figure out what to do next. "Where am I taking you?"

"Wherever it is you think you're going."

"I need to be alone. To think. Alone."

"Too damn bad, girl. You're not going to be alone for one damn minute until we figure out who the hell is behind these attempts on your life. Don't like it, I don't give a shit. Be pissed all you want but I'll be glued to your side. Get used to it."

Is that all it took to get me all hot and bothered? A hot biker bossing me around?

Sadly, yes it was.

"Say you understand, Vivi."

I turned to Jag with a pissed off look. "You understand, Vivi."

He smirked. "Smart ass."

# Chapter Thirteen

*Jag*

Since Vivi wasn't eager to give me all the details of what the fuck was going on, I decided to do some digging on my own. I knew Roadkill had a few guys who did freelance wet work, but I still couldn't find any connection to any of those assholes and Governor Blaise. Three hours and I couldn't find shit. Less than shit and the person who had all the answers was two feet away from me. Vivi sat beside me with expensive white and gold headphones blaring a tinny guitar sound and that was the only sound she made. Other than the rapid click of her fingers over the keyboard.

"You're staring." She didn't look up and her fingers never stopped. "Stop."

"I'm not staring. I'm trying to see what you're doing." I laid my head on her shoulder and chuckled when she tried to shove me away. "What are you doing?"

"Working. What are you doing?"

"Trying to get this stubborn woman to tell me what she's hiding from me."

"What a bitch," she deadpanned and turned the volume up on her music. I would have pushed the issue, but the doorbell rang.

I wasn't expecting any company and I didn't think anyone in Vivi's life knew where she was. Then again, I had no idea if she even had anyone in her life. "I'll get that, don't worry yourself."

"I won't," she shouted over the music in her ears.

"What's so funny," Gunnar asked when I opened the door with a chuckle, his adorable little sister smiling up at me from her car seat.

"Nothing. Come on in."

"Thanks. Take this," he shoved a frilly looking diaper bag into my arms with a grunt. "Damn kid needs a lot of shit."

"Wait until she's a teenager."

## HEAVENLY HACKED

"Yeah, thanks for that asshole."

"Anytime. Beer? Should you be drinking with a kid?"

Gunnar grunted again and set the baby carrier down on the coffee table. "I don't drink with her. She watches me drink and I wipe her ass. It's kind of our thing."

"So?"

"Beer me," he said, bent over his sister and removing at least ten thousand different straps that kept her safe in that wicked contraption.

I was already on my way to the kitchen. "Any preference?"

"Something dark," he shouted back.

"What about you, Vivi?"

"She's gone," Gunnar called out, sounding amused.

With two beers in hand, I went back to the living room and found that Vivi had slipped out. "She say anything?"

"Not one word."

Figured. I wasn't worried that she'd run off, mostly because I had her key fob. And her steering wheel. "What brings you by?"

"Cross says he might have a lead on those burned out pot fields. Needs you to dig and see if you can find any link to Roadkill." Cross had been sure it was Roadkill MC from the start, but we had no proof. Yet. "Just do your digital voodoo shit."

"I'm on it. How are things going with Maisie?" I nodded to the little girl, kicking and squirming in her seat when Gunnar picked her up and plunked her my arms.

"Being a single parent is hard as fuck, man. I give respect to women who do this shit, but I get it. She's adorable and I fell in love with her the minute Mom put her in my arms. Every day something is different."

Gunnar sighed and his shoulders fell. "It would be nice if I could find someone trustworthy and not afraid of the MC to look after her."

That was a problem for pretty much everything when you were in an MC. Girlfriends, housekeepers and any other personal care help was hard to come by because people feared the lifestyle. Feared retaliation from criminal wrongdoing and all other variety of bullshit that had no bearing on our lives. Mostly. "You need a professional agency or a personal recommendation."

"Yeah thanks, Sherlock. I just need to fucking find someone but enough talking about me. How are things with you and Vivi?"

I took a long pull from my beer and told him what I knew. And what I didn't. "She thinks I'm either working the government against her, or with Roadkill, but I can't figure out how they're involved or why she even thinks they are." It was getting under my fucking skin that she wouldn't tell me. Hell, she shared my bed but couldn't share this.

"Do what you gotta do to find out, man. It could help figure out what the fuck Roadkill has been up to." I knew Gunnar wasn't trying to be a mercenary, that the club always came first. But it still pissed me off. "And the bullet in the windshield of that hippie mobile?"

I'd told him about our escape from the stakeout. "Another story involving Vivi spying on Roadkill at their HQ." I wanted to be pissed off at her, but she probably had a point that my presence hadn't helped in that situation. "Can't confirm or deny it was Roadkill but it's a safe bet."

Gunnar nodded thoughtfully but I knew what was on his mind. He wanted me to do whatever it took to get that information from Vivi. And I would but it would be on my own time. "Keep her close. And get that info however you can."

"It doesn't work that like with Vivi." A guy like Gunnar wouldn't understand because he was a black and white kind of guy.

## HEAVENLY HACKED

"I thought you said you didn't know her." Ignoring his accusatory tone, I switched Maisie into my other arm.

"Not since we were kids but there are some things I do know about her and this is one of them. If she doesn't trust me then I won't be able to trust any info she gives me. Bad intel is worse than no intel at all."

"Then make her trust you," he insisted.

I glared his way. "Hire a damned nanny."

Gunnar's scowled deepened before morphing into a smile. "Easier to say, right?"

I nodded and turned Maisie around to face me. She was so damn cute, it made me wonder if I'd ever have kids of my own. I figured it was unlikely, but I still had plenty of time to worry about that. For now I just enjoyed the feel of the baby in my arms. "You can always come stare at my handsome face when your brother's ugly mug gets to be too much." She grinned, kicking her chubby little legs as she kissed my nose, though in fairness it felt more like she was gnawing on it, but I didn't care. Not even when drool ran down my face.

"You wish. No man will stack up to all this."

We shared a laugh but soon Maisie began to fall asleep and Gunnar stood to leave. "I'll get with Cross tomorrow if I find anything."

He nodded and strapped the little girl back into her prison and lifted the seat and the bag. "Sounds good. Get that intel, Jag."

As soon as Gunnar was gone, my shoulders relaxed. He had me feeling tense and angry and I didn't like it. Dammit. But there was something, or rather, someone else on my mind and I went in search of her.

The garage and the camper were quiet. Too quiet, so I knocked. Vivi didn't answer but I knew she was in there because all the doors and windows were locked. I knocked harder. "Open up, Vivi! I know you're in there!" She still didn't answer and after a few minutes, I gave up.

## HEAVENLY HACKED

About an hour later, I was in my own lab digging through Roadkill MC records, and a text came through from Vivi.

*Come back later. For sex.*

I laughed and got back to work until the elusive *later* arrived.

\*\*\*

Vivi crept into my bed, crawling up from the foot, dotting soft kisses along my skin. She tried to be quiet, stealthy, but I heard her the second she opened the garage door. I guessed her *later* was sooner than I thought. I heard her as she crept up the stairs, but it was more fun to see what she had planned than to interrupt her.

Her lips touched down on my abs, my hips and up to my pecs where she swiped a tongue across each nipple and it took all of my willpower to keep quiet. That mouth kept crawling up, licking across my collarbone and up my neck until she nibbled my bottom lip and kissed her way over to my ear. "I like this game. Let's keep it up and see how long it takes you to admit you're awake."

That was my moment, to give up but I couldn't. My jaws clamped tight when her tongue swirled around my earlobe before her teeth dug into my skin. Her laugh was deep and husky as tension snaked its way through my body, and then she fell silent again. The only sound was my heavy breathing, the quiet sound of her lips on my skin, moving down my chest, my abs as she quickly tugged on the waistband of my boxers. My cock was already semi-hard in her hands and getting harder with every slide up and down. The friction was driving me out of my fucking mind. "Ah, shit!"

Her tongue slicked across the slit of my cock and my hips bucked off the bed. She laughed and wrapped her mouth around my cock, sucking like a lollipop at first, using her lips and tongue to drive me crazy. Vivi had issued the challenge and I needed to be the victor but her mouth was a lethal weapon and would be the instrument of my demise.

"Mmm," she moaned as she slid her lips slowly down the length of my cock until it hit the back of her throat and my body went tight again. Another laugh escaped, vibrating all around me. She did it again, took me so deep I couldn't stop my body's reaction to her. And her mouth.

"Fuck, Vivi." She swallowed around me and the friction sent a shiver of greedy desire through me. Her throat closing around the tip of my cock was all I needed to lose control. "Shit," I groaned and thrust up into her mouth.

She grinned up at me, her gray eyes never leaving mine as she fucked me with her mouth, keeping my dick stiff and standing straight up. Another dare lit her gaze as she crossed her arms behind her back, daring me to fuck that pouty little mouth of hers. I wasn't an animal, but a man could only take so much.

I couldn't look away from the way she stuck her tongue out so the underside of my cock got increased friction with every stroke. Her eyes darkened, transformed as I fucked her mouth and slid my cock against her tongue. Melted gunmetal peered back at me, wicked with mischief as she dared me to lose control. "You getting' wet Vivi, sucking me off?"

She nodded, taking me so deep my hips jerked on their own and she moaned.

"Fuck me," she moaned. From deepthroating my cock.

"Vivi." My hips began to move faster and faster and a voice in the back of my mind told me to slow down but I couldn't. I was physically unable to stop fucking her mouth.

"Do it," she dared me, her mouth around my dick as if she knew my control was close to snapping.

My fingertips barely held her as I cradled her face, stroking deep into her mouth and down her throat, moaning at the way she kept swallowing around me, adding more tongue and more moisture to send me out of my fucking mind.

"Fucking mouth," I growled, strokes coming faster and deeper and then her name was on my lips as I shot my load onto her tongue and into her throat. My body jerked violently and Vivi, the little tease, didn't let up at all. Her tongue and lips kept up a steady torture until every last aftershock left my body.

"That mouth of yours is trouble in more ways than one," I said on a chuckle.

She laughed and released me with a pop. "I didn't hear any complaints."

"Fuck no and you won't. Now I know the perfect way to shut you up." Before she could take another breath, I switched our position so my hips and my cock were cradled between her thighs.

Vivi's creamy legs tightened around my waist. "Are you here for decoration or purpose?"

"Yes," I told her, fisting my cock in my hand and pumping it twice before I pushed into her. "Fuck you're always so fucking wet."

"You might have something to do with that," she purred back, pussy already fluttering with greed around me. My cock wasn't fully erect yet, but her pussy dripped between us and he was almost there. She let out a sexy little gasp and I sank deep. Nine inches deep and growing hard as fuck. "Jag," she moaned and swirled her hips. "More. Fuck me," she whispered.

My control snapped at her words, her gritty command and I grabbed her ankles, placing them on my shoulders so I could sink even deeper into her hot, waiting body. My hips took on a mind of their own, pounding with a blind devotion I couldn't describe.

"Jag, yes! Oh fuck yeah," she shouted. "Please," she said, gripping me close even while she tried to crawl away from me, and what a fucking heady feeling that was. Vivi's walls clamped down hard at first, a jarringly violent motion that turned into tiny flutters that vibrated all around my cock while I mindlessly pounded into her.

Her body flooded with moisture and I fucked her harder, hypnotized by the way her creamy tits bounced with every stroke. And then another orgasm crashed over her, milking me until I was bone dry. Her name was on my lips once again as I emptied myself into her.

"Fuck, Vivi." I collapsed on top of her, chest heaving but I couldn't move away. She smelled too good and she felt too damn good.

Her laughter echoed in the room. "Gimme a few minutes and I will."

Her words made me grin and I rolled off her, pulling her close and we fell asleep with our bodies still intertwined.

# Chapter Fourteen

*Vivi*

"Un-fucking-believable!" Not only wasn't the good Governor keeping a low profile while he had people trying to kill me, but the asshole was planning a big fucking fundraiser. Here in Las Vegas at some hotel owned by a rich and handsome one percenter. At twenty-five grand a plate it wasn't worth attending just to get up in his grill, but that didn't mean I couldn't still fuck with him. I brewed a full pot of coffee in Jag's kitchen and began working on my plan.

Vengeance, if nothing else, would be my final act.

But before any of that could happen it was time to shit or get off the proverbial pot. A disgusting phrase I'd always hated until that alert sounded on my phone. If I was going to be brave enough to go balls to the wall against a sitting governor or a crazed gangster, then I needed to decide who I could trust and who I couldn't. Starting with Jag.

If I decided he wasn't on the up and up with me, then I needed to walk away. Forget him. If I chose to put my faith in him, then I had to trust him fully. With everything. And I had to be absolutely certain that trust wasn't based on the fact that he was dicking me good whenever he got the chance. And the dick *was* good, amazing even, so I had to make this decision with a clear head. Logic and reason were my friends and they said Jag could help me with his tech and badass military biker skills. And if I was wrong, well I was dead anyway, wasn't I?

But a pot of coffee and a long hot shower later, I had my answer and I was resolute. In my decision, if not execution.

"I was wondering if you were hiding or avoiding me?"

I turned from my computer to see him draped casually against the doorjamb like some Nubian god. Way to disrupt my concentration, Jag. "Avoiding you? Didn't I just spend all night wrapped around you and sucking you off?"

## HEAVENLY HACKED

Even trying to play it casual had my body responding to the memories of Jag in my mouth, my pussy. His big hands all over my body.

"You were up there for a long time, especially considering you killed an entire pot of coffee." For emphasis he held up the coffee pot with maybe a swallow of brown liquid in it and swirled it around, but my attention was on his smooth mahogany skin. Other than one puckered scar low on the right side of his back, his skin was so smooth it looked liquid. Lickable.

"You want me to make another pot for you?"

He turned, one eyebrow arched in that cocky way that made me want to smack him or kiss him. Maybe both. "No. I'm fine."

"You hungry?"

"If you can put some warm butter and maple syrup together, I'll pretend I'm starved."

Jag turned with a proud smile. "Well you did get quite the cardio workout last night."

I took a seat at the kitchen table and crossed my legs. "Don't you have a job to go to?" Yeah, I was stalling but I had a plan. Sort of.

"I do but I took some time off to take care of you. Remember the whole not leaving your side thing?"

"You were serious?" I groaned and rolled my eyes.

"I was serious," he said, dark chocolate pecs just inches from my suddenly watering mouth. Was that due to the muscles or the pancakes he'd started to make? Who the hell knew or cared?

"Go in to work today, Jag. I'll come with you and hang out at the shop. You have wi-fi there, don't you?"

By way of an answer he slid a plate full of heaven at me. "Eat."

"Okay!" He didn't have to tell me twice. The pancakes were fluffy and just sweet enough to need nothing but a pat of butter and the bacon was crispy, fatty and delicious. How did he put that together so fast? Had I been drooling over him without noticing it?

## HEAVENLY HACKED

"I thought you wanted to go into the shop," he bit out and I looked up, confused.

"I do. But, you're not even finished eating yet."

He smirked. "And I won't get to if you don't stop making noises while you eat that make my dick hard, Vivi."

Damn I love the way he said my name, like it was an oath or a prayer. No wonder women lost their shit over certain men.

I pushed my plate away. Breakfast was getting complicated as shit. "I'll go get my stuff and meet you outside." I was pretty sure he mumbled "thank fuck" as I left the kitchen, but I decided not to call him on it. The man was trying to help after all.

I hoped.

***

We were inside GET INK'D for nearly an hour when Jag finally muttered, "Why in the hell did I listen to you? We could have stayed home and gotten all blissed out in my big bed. I haven't had one customer all day." He glared at me and I pretended to be engrossed in a book on my tablet.

"Feel free to go out there and drum up some business," Golden Boy, the owner said to him, catching him by surprise. Behind us, Lasso laughed so hard his broad shoulders shook.

"I'm good, thanks. But we're leaving soon," he said with his unhappy gaze aimed my way.

I shrugged but the chimes over the door sounded before I could come up with a smartass comment and a group of four well-dressed women walked in wearing bachelorette sashes.

"Hello honey," the leader of the pack said to Golden Boy. "Do you work here?" Her sweet southern accent was thick and cultured.

"Nope. They're keeping me here against my will."

With a hand to her chest the woman laughed prettily. "Lucky you. I hear these boys are h-o-t hot! Anyone back there?"

Jag came out first with Lasso right behind him. "How can I help you ladies?"

"My goodness but you do grow 'em big here don'tcha? I'm the bride and I want a piercing."

Jag smiled. "You'll have to be more specific than that, lady."

Her eyes flashed appreciation. "I want my clit pierced. That specific enough for ya, sugar?"

"Yep. But ah," Jag rubbed his neck and I held my breath, waiting to see what he'd say. Though the woman was braced for the worst, I didn't think that was the kind of man Jeremiah had grown into.

"Spit it out, big guy."

"Well it says you're the bride, so I assume that means you're getting married soon?"

She nodded, arms crossed in a stance that said she would fight if she had to. "And you have a problem with that?"

"For fuck's sake lady, your clit might not be healed in time for your honeymoon!"

I sucked in a breath at the same time she did. But before I could recover, the southern belle beamed a smile at him. "That's mighty sweet of you, mister. Let's go with the nipples then?"

"Come on back and I'll get you started on the paperwork."

"Make this one yours, honey!" said her friend. With more swing in her hips than I could ever produce on purpose, she followed Jag to the back with one friend and the others stepped outside to vape.

I might have stared at the space Jag occupied a bit too long but dammit he really was a good guy. A biker, sure. A hacker, too, and some type of government contractor like me, but he was still one of the good ones and that scene just proved it. The last thing I needed was to renew my crush on Jag, but the man was making it damn hard.

Damn hard.

# HEAVENLY HACKED

"So you do like him," Lasso said, breaking into my thoughts.

"Of course I do, we used to be friends."

He shrugged. "Not for a long time."

And that was exactly the reminder I needed to take that crush and send it straight to hell. "Yeah well he's the one who left. Not me." And this time it would be me who left.

"Really?"

"Really." I turned back to my tablet because the last fucking thing I wanted to think about was how many people in my life find it so easy to walk away. Too easy, if you ask me. Which they never did.

Twenty minutes later Jag came out with the woman, looking mentally exhausted. When the shop was empty again I smiled at him. "Got room for another customer?"

"You?"

"Me. I want to add some color and shading to my feathers." He smiled at the mention of his favorite tattoo that he traced most nights until I fell asleep in his arms.

"Come on."

"Clean the room when you're done. Thoroughly," Lasso called out with a snicker.

We both ignored him and I followed Jag into one of the rooms with a door instead of a curtain. Normally I would have given him a hard time for being presumptuous but the talk I wanted to have would be better in private.

He gestured to the table. "Hop up."

I watched him gather his tools, mesmerized by the play of muscles in his forearms and biceps.

I got comfortable on the table, the slick paper crunching under my ass, and began to lift the hem of my shirt when his hand shot out to stop me. "What?" I complained.

## HEAVENLY HACKED

"I'll do it." A playful smile curled his lips and I played along, letting him adjust my clothes as needed until he crooned, "Perfect," in my ear.

"Hardly," I snorted and then the room was filled with the buzz of the tattoo gun. And only the sounds of the tattoo gun. Tats made me squirmy, and they hurt like hell, so I broke the silence to relieve me of the nerves. "Tell me about the relationship the Reckless Bastards have with Roadkill?"

He stilled and the tattoo gun went silent. "Why?"

"Because I'd like to know, if you don't mind telling me."

He said nothing for a long time and I kept my back to him. When the gun started up again, I had my answer. "We tolerate each other, or at least we used to until recently. When White Boy Craig took over as Prez, shit went crazy over there and they got into some bad shit. We co-existed as much as it was possible but then little things started to happen. A burnt pot field and then teaming up with outsiders to go after one of our women. Now I'd say we're edging close to war."

*War.*

He said the word with such ease for a man who knew the realities of war. I turned, risking a glance because I wanted to see his eyes as he said those words. I needed to see him. The words hadn't been spoken lightly. War. That's when I made up my mind.

I told him, "There was another photo. Two more actually. Two FBI agents with a man who looks like a gangster, V. Rizzoli which I'm pretty sure is the VP of Roadkill."

The gun stopped again and moved away from my skin. "Why tell me this now?"

I sighed and turned away. "I'm choosing to trust you, Jag."

He stood and walked around the chair, crouching down so we were face to face. "Why?"

"Because if you're working with them, I'm dead anyway."

## Chapter Fifteen

*Jag*

Fuck!

Two days after Vivi spilled her guts to me at GET INK'D, I could still only utter one word. Fuck. Shit was so much more fucked up than I realized in Vivi's life. Not only did she have a high level politician with a lot to lose if anyone found out about him chasing after his underage girlfriend, probably with hired government and private goons on Vivi's tail, but now there was also Vigo.

Vigo wasn't just the Vice President of Roadkill MC, he was a psychopathic son of a bitch who got off on causing people pain. He volunteered for the wet work and I was pretty sure the guy moonlighted as a serial killer. To put it short, he was batshit fucking crazy and if he was also an FBI informant he was likely to act bold. Reckless.

That meant Vivi was in even more trouble than she knew. And I had to be the one to tell her. Fuck!

Vivi breezed into the living room wearing her standard skintight black jeans and a dark tank top, only today she was barefoot. It probably didn't mean a damn thing other than she'd been so engrossed in whatever angle she was working today and had forgotten to put on her boots. It didn't mean she was comfortable here. Or that she was staying. "I have something for you."

I smiled at her and patted the seat beside me. "I love surprises," I told her even though I didn't. Surprises were rarely good but when she sat I palmed her thigh. "What is it?"

"It's not that, dirty boy." Vivi pushed my hands away and turned the laptop so I could see the screen but I pulled her closer and kept the computer where it was.

"That's better. Now show me."

## HEAVENLY HACKED

"Okay look." She showed me several tabs of emails from Rizzoli to Agent Ryan. "They both thought they were being so careful, but this is an old school trick that even teenage girls used to talk to older guys online. Rizzoli wrote an email to Agent Ryan but instead of sending it, he saved it to the drafts folder and when Agent Ryan replied he did the same." Vivi slid the laptop to my lap and stood. "Check out the drafts written in early May last year."

I did what she said but, of course, Vivi had already pulled them up. "Motherfucker!" Rizzoli, that crazy fucker, had sent an email to the feds the day before the pot field had been set on fire. *Lookout for retaliation by the Bastards. Burned marijuana fields.* "I'm going to kill that motherfucker myself."

"I know." She sat and put a 2-liter bottle of diet root beer on the table along with two plastic tumblers full of ice. "I debated whether or not to share this with you, Jag. Because I know what it means." She poured the root beer into each glass and handed one to me, her eyes serious as they tore through me. "War. Another war for you." Vivi took a drink and sighed, as though the thought of me going back to war was hard to take. "I also know that the more wars you fight, the better the odds are of you dying."

"Hey, Vivi, it'll be fine."

"No it won't," she shot back. "You don't know that it'll be fine and we both know that much, but this decision wasn't mine to make. So here." She handed me a flash drive. "To share with your club."

"Shit Vivi, thank you." I didn't know how to express just how much this meant to me, getting exactly what we needed without any games.

"Don't thank me for this, Jag. I wanted like hell to keep this from you. To scrub it from my drives and pretend I never saw any of it, but if you have to fight, then I prefer knowing you're going in prepared. Or at least that you know there is a fight." Her gray eyes were suspiciously wet and that just fucking gutted me. My tough girl, eyes wet with tears. For me.

## HEAVENLY HACKED

I didn't deserve her tears and that only made them impact me even more. "Aw, you care about me," I joked.

"No need to make a big deal out of it," she grumbled. "I'll be in my camper."

I wanted to stop her, to go after her and show her just how grateful I was that she'd come through for the club but she needed space. I didn't know what changed over the past few days, but she'd been quieter than usual and spent more time in her trailer. I hated it, but she'd already had so much change and upheaval, I couldn't begrudge her time and space.

So much fucking space I was suffocating with it but armed with the info from Vivi, there was no fucking time to waste. I picked up my phone and pressed the Prez's number. "Cross, I got the info you need. Concrete proof, man."

"Fuck yeah. You on your way here?" Ever since Lauren died Cross was always at the clubhouse. I didn't even know if he ever went back to the house they shared or if he even still owned that house.

"Vivi's here and I can't leave her alone."

"Shit. Can't you bring her with?" I understood his frustration, but I doubted she would agree.

"Probably not but I'll see what I can do, man."

"Thanks, Jag. Really."

"Don't thank me, it was Vivi who found it. I'll keep you posted." The call ended, and I tossed my phone on the table beside Vivi's empty tumbler. Vivi. Having her here was surreal but in the best way possible. I just wish she wasn't in so much fucking danger.

Now all I wanted to do was to keep her safe and sound.

# Chapter Sixteen

*Vivi*

There were a dozen bikes parked outside of Jag's house, which meant just one thing: a meeting of the Reckless Bastards going on inside. I didn't know what that meant exactly, but I was pretty sure it had something to do with Vigo Rizzoli. I fucking hated giving Jag that info but he was the only one who could decide how to fight. Whether to fight.

Of course he would fight. They all would. And someone might die. I just hoped it wasn't Jag. Since I had no control over any of that, I focused on the layout of Siren Casino and Resort. Blaise's campaign had reserved the grand ballroom but a prominent billionaire had paid the tab. Charitable donation, my ass. Still it was good to know where he would be and when because it gave me time to plot my revenge. Even if I wasn't around to enjoy it, that motherfucker would know.

"Pack a bag Vivi!" Jag pounded on my door. "Be quick!"

I rolled my eyes and continued to eye the blueprints. Drake Foster had good cyber security at his place. It just wasn't good enough. Getting in had been easy and so far, no one had been alerted that there was a breach in security. "Where am I going?"

I jumped a little when Jag's hand smacked the door again. "Dammit, Vivi."

I took a few screen grabs of the blueprints and shut my computer before opening the door. Lasso stood behind him but I fixed my glare just on Jag. "I am not a child, Jag. Don't bark orders at me. Tell me what's going on."

He sighed and stepped up, getting in my space until I backed away. "Me and Cross need to go take care of some things and I can't leave you alone. I won't," he amended to stop me from arguing.

"Where am I going? Exactly, Jag."

"Lasso's place. His wife is pregnant so he's staying behind and—"

"I don't think so. Fuck that."

"Aw, c'mon sugar. I thought we were gettin' along," Lasso said.

I groaned. "You're fine, cowboy. But you have a pregnant wife at home and I have people trying to kill me. Do I really need to do the math for you?"

He frowned and stepped into the camper to scowl at me, shrinking the space even further. "You sayin' I can't take care of you and my wife?"

"I'm saying the people who are after me won't give a shit if she's pregnant and has nothing to do with this." I turned away and grabbed another pair of jeans and stuffed some other junk into a bag. "I'll stay someplace else but not with you and not with anyone else. Enough people are in danger already."

Jag butted in about then. "Dammit, Vivi, don't make this difficult. Just go with Lasso. He'll keep you safe. Hang out with Rocky and let her feed you. It's one fuckin' night."

"Don't use reason to sway me, damn you."

He laughed and I rolled my eyes. "If anything happens, you protect her first. I can handle myself, contrary to what some people around here think." I aimed that barb at Jag.

He stepped forward. "Vivi, I know you can handle yourself."

I turned to Lasso. "Give us a minute."

He nodded and stepped out, saying, "Grab your helmet 'cause I didn't bring an extra one."

Jag pulled the door shut. "Vivi, I know you are more than capable of taking care of yourself but if you think for one second these guys will come at you one at a time, you're wrong. Plus I won't be any good to my club, or my brothers knowing you're here on your own."

## HEAVENLY HACKED

"You don't fight fair."

He flashed his beautiful smile again. It always made my tongue tingle with a desire to get a taste of it.

"No, I don't. But I need to be able to focus. I need you to go with Lasso."

"Fine. I'll go." I didn't want Jag or any of his friends getting hurt because he was worried about me. "Don't do anything stupid."

"We won't. This is just a pickup but we're going through some unfriendly areas. I'll be back tomorrow in time for a late dinner." Jag hesitated for a second, but his mouth was on mine again and all I could think about was this man. Everything about him was good and I wondered if I could ever live in his world.

Plus he was sexy as hell, and those taut muscles were a personal weakness of mine. Just like the man, his kisses electrified my senses like they were being caressed by live wire.

"I already said I'd go, but I'm not above a little bribery now and again."

He smirked. "Good to know." When he stepped back my body rejected the cool air and the distance now between us. "See you soon, Vivi. Be good."

"Why would I when it's so much fun being bad?"

\*\*\*

"It's official," Rocky said giving me one of her infectious laughs. "Any woman who can scare that big cowboy into hiding is my new favorite person."

Rocky was a sassy redhead who talked like a cheerleader and dressed like a hippie. When I arrived last night she refused to let me wallow in my sullen mood, using compliments and then insults to get me to talk to her. She hadn't stopped talking since.

"He's not scared of me, just tired of my bitching. Not that I'm not appreciative of your hospitality or anything because I am. It's just that, I don't really stay at people's houses."

She blinked big green eyes and sat back, rubbing her belly. "Never? Not even a girlfriend or anything?"

"Nope. I left home when I was a kid and used my computer skills to get an apartment and pay my bills, which meant I didn't have time for things like girlfriends and sleepovers." I was glad Rocky didn't look at me with pity because I hated that.

"So how'd you meet Jag? Lasso said you were his online girlfriend."

That pulled a laugh out of me. "That's how he would put it but we were just friends. We met online and talked and chatted. Only online. I met him for the first time now, when I got to Vegas."

"That's so cool. I don't have any friends from Florida. I was too busy helping my dad plan bank robberies."

Even though I could hear the pain in her voice, the wistfulness for a different, more idyllic childhood, I didn't pity her. She'd moved past it and made a life for herself.

"Not as cool as it sounds, right?"

"Too right." She stood and rubbed her belly. "Hungry?"

"Uh yeah, but I'm pretty sure you should be lying in a bed surrounded by pillows. Sit down, I can do it."

"You cook too?" she said, heading for the kitchen and unloading the refrigerator.

I frowned at the disbelief in her voice. "I can't cook? I can read instructions and follow them better than anyone. Besides I used to dabble in a bit of chemistry."

"Just remember I got a pregnant nose."

I didn't know what the hell that meant but I stood and stared at all the things Rocky had lined up on the counter. "I take it that you can have all of these things on the counter?"

"Yep."

I diced mushrooms and onions and peppers, whipped up eggs and slid bacon into the oven. It was a mechanical sort of activity, cooking. The perfect thing to do when I needed to stop thinking and just let my mind work in the background on a solution. "Sorry, I'm not a chatty cooker."

"That's okay. Are you really a badass hacker babe? Lasso's words, not mine."

Lasso was such a guy's guy, so alpha yet so well-meaning it was hard to take offense. "I wouldn't say I'm any of those things. But I do have mad computer skills that I use for good and for evil, but not too evil and only if the price is right." I shook my head as an ironic laugh bubbled out of me. "And to think, it's not the shady jobs that sent me on the run. How'd you end up with a cowboy biker?"

She laughed and shook her head. "Actually, it was a one night stand. He was in San Diego for a wedding and I was catering the reception. He was charming and stepped in when a few of my ex's goons got a bit too handsy. One thing led to another and we had the most amazing night together. Like you, I ran to him when trouble fell in my lap."

Damn. That was kind of cool but when I thought about what that could possibly mean for me, I froze. "Good for you," I said uncomfortably.

Like she'd read my mind she breezed on. "It might not happen, but I'm pretty sure it will," she said with a smug smile. "Lasso's never seen Jag serious about a girl. A woman, sorry."

"Jag isn't serious about me, Rocky. We're old friends and he's a good guy who wants to help me out. If anything, he probably feels bad that he ghosted me." Which was something I needed to keep in mind whenever my thoughts became a little too fanciful.

Rocky gave me a side-eye and said, "I don't think so, but I can see you're hardheaded. Plus I'm hardly going to lecture someone who took my weak ass breakfast and turned it into a feast. Me and baby thank you." She dug in before I could even grab a chair, but I wasn't judging. Sharing meals with another person was a rarity, so I tried to enjoy it.

"Not a feast. Eat up."

## HEAVENLY HACKED

She picked up her phone, typed a message and put it down before picking up her fork. "Your eggs are way fluffier than mine. What did you add?"

"Salt and pepper. I just cooked them on a lower heat so they get fluffy as they cook instead of flat."

The bedroom door opened down the hall and Lasso's heavy footsteps sounded on the floor. "Somebody said breakfast?"

"Have a seat. Look at all this food Vivi made for us! The baby is super happy!" Rocky even did a little dance as she ate, wiggling her hips with each bite.

"Thanks. You didn't poison mine did you?"

"I didn't have time to pack it on such short notice."

He stared at me and then burst out laughing. "Yeah, you're exactly what a serious dude like Jag needs."

"I'm not what anybody needs." I stabbed my eggs and ignored the stares between him and Rocky. "We used to be friends, that's it."

"Bullshit. But you're scared, I get it. I was too, that's why I married my baby before she could run away. Didn't fall for her until later."

Rocky frowned. "I thought you said you fell in love with me in San Diego?" Her eyes twinkled with mischief.

"Of course I did, babe. But later, when we were running for our lives that love changed. Grew up. Matured. My point, Vivi, is that you should be scared. Love is serious business."

"Who the hell said anything about love?" I stood and got more coffee. "Just because you're all coupled up and happy doesn't mean everyone is headed that way. I have work to do." With that, I stormed into the guest room feeling like a fucking child.

A petulant child.

# Chapter Seventeen

*Jag*

The ride up to Tahoe had been uneventful and the transaction with our weapons guy was just how I liked these things to go, quick and easy. There was no drama, no changing of terms and no attempts at bullshit. He got our money and we got our guns loaded up in the van and were on our way in less than an hour.

But Cross wanted to talk strategy so we stopped for dinner at an all-night diner somewhere in Reno instead of driving straight back. I could admit that I was eager to get back to Vivi because I wanted to see her and no other reason, which made me sound like a fucking lovesick teenager.

"So we know what our options are," Cross began when the adolescent waitress brought our burgers and fries. "The question is, do we want war?"

Savior snorted. "Sorry Prez but the question isn't do we want it, it's can we afford it? We have businesses to worry about, women and some of us have families to think about, too. We're not kids anymore, Cross."

The expression that flashed on Cross's face was deadly, but it was gone as fast as it had appeared. "Yeah, that's how time works, Savior. But this is about the club, not what we all have to lose personally." It was a shitty thing that people didn't want to hear, but Cross was the President and it was his job to think about the club. Not just our club but the whole Reckless Bastards Organization, which would all be threatened by war.

"I hear ya, but the facts are facts." Savior, once the biggest dog of all of us, had softened when he'd fallen for a fallen brother's younger sister. "I'll do what I have to do but we need to make sure this is the best option."

## HEAVENLY HACKED

"I agree with Savior," Max said. His deep gruff voice always sounded a little rusty because he was so damn quiet. "Do we have any other options?"

We had a few options but before we could discuss them any further, a table full of frat boys settled in next to us. It was one thing to discuss club business inside a public, but deserted, restaurant but it was unheard of to do it where anyone might overhear. Especially this kind of information.

"I could use a smoke," Savior said. The rest of us got up from the table with him, dropping a few bills on the table before we filed out. By the time we caught up with him, Savior had a half finished cigarette hanging between his lips. "Come on, Jag. Let's hear it."

"Cross could slip these photos to the Roadkill Prez and let them deal with him."

"But we run the risk that they already know what he's doing to cover their asses and we tip our hand," Max said, shocking the shit out of all of us. Not with his idea but with his use of all the words.

"Exactly," I told him. "Though that's unlikely since the meetings and communication have all been clandestine. Or we can prod them into doing some shit the feds won't be able to ignore. Get rid of them for good." That was my preference but Vivi's shimmering gray eyes kept playing behind in my mind. The tortured sound of her voice as she talked about the costs of war stayed with me. Maybe it would be better to let Roadkill handle their own shit.

"I suppose you have a plan for that?" Cross sounded more amused than annoyed but there was definitely some annoyance there.

"Not yet but give me a few days and I might." A short nod was about as good as it would get from Cross right now and I didn't need his validation. Not on this.

"When you do, I'll be ready to listen." Cross stood tall among us, carrying himself apart from us. Not on purpose but as the leader he was responsible for everything and everyone. The burden hung heaviest on him but he never complained.

# HEAVENLY HACKED

We spent a few hours dicking around at a casino while a couple prospects watched the van filled with guns and after a few cups of coffee, we were all back on the road. The drive wasn't long, about six hours and it was nice to just let my bike go for a while. Not that my mind was clear at all, it wasn't. I couldn't stop thinking of all the things that could go wrong for me. The Club. Vivi.

Even as the road became a blur as I rode behind Cross and right beside Max, my mind wouldn't shut the fuck up. Vivi was in real danger and there was a good chance I'd be too deep in club shit to protect her. I hoped it didn't come to that. I really fucking did.

But we were close to home which meant I would soon have Vivi in my arms. In my bed.

Lights flashed behind us, drawing my attention. In the mirror I could only see Savior's lights flashing, a sign that something was wrong. I raised a hand to let him know I saw him and then I moved closer to Max to get his attention. "Something's up!"

He nodded and fell back, leaving me to pull up beside Cross to let him know we had trouble. But the moment our front wheels aligned a bullet whizzed by my head. The sound was unmistakable, even through the muffled noise of my helmet and the engine revving at close to eighty miles an hour. "Shots?"

I nodded and pulled back again, reaching for my own firearm. It could be dangerous, carrying a firearm over state lines but we had an out of the way spot where we met with our contact so if cops came sniffing around it would be because someone had dropped the dime on us. And that only made me think about Rizzoli and those feds. Something still didn't feel right about that but now wasn't the time to wonder.

Another bullet flew by but this time the source was clear. The shooter was behind us. There was a curve up ahead which could give us time to put some distance between us, or it could slow us down and sign our death warrants.

"Gun it," I yelled to Cross while I pulled off the to the side of the road and dismounted. Max stayed right with me, finding cover behind a boulder as Savior hung back and positioned himself behind the fucking lowrider and the two bikes behind it, which put him between the van with our shipment of guns and those assholes.

"Ready?" Max's deadly serious expression lit with awareness, with that focus all former servicemembers got when the game was back on. Shoulders squared, Max pulled a handgun from his holster and dropped down on knee.

"Fuck yeah." I leaned on the other side of my bike, using the seat to line up my shots as I heard the bikes approaching. "You take the first fucker and I'll handle the second."

Max nodded and turned his focus to the road. I hated to say it, but this reminded me of my days in the military in the best way possible. Honing in on a target with razor sharp focus, letting nothing else distract you. Not thoughts of home nor gray-eyed girls. Not the fly buzzing around your ear nor the glint of sun doing its best to blind you. The only thing that mattered was the target. Whether ten feet or a thousand feet, the target was the priority.

The roar of the bike engine purred and whined as they rounded the bend, gunning it to catch up with the bikes they expected to see. The sound of Max's shot pierced the air, followed seconds later by mine. Both bikes went down, sending the riders skidding across the pavement.

Savior pulled up the rear, making room for our guys to pass unharmed before doubling back to the assholes laid out on the asphalt. Max stood and drew closer to the other one and I had his six, sweeping the landscape in search of more shooters while keeping an eye on the felled drivers.

"What do you see?"

"Roadkill pieces of shit," Savior said, spitting on the one closest to him. "What were you hoping to accomplish asshole?"

"Max?" I shouted.

# HEAVENLY HACKED

"Same," he called out with a grunt and a second later a shot rang out. "Son of a bitch! That fucker shot me."

My feet were on the move, drawing closer to Max who stood with one hand cupping his shoulder. "Talk to me, Max."

"I'm fine, the fucking thing just grazed me. Surprised me is all."

Savior rushed over and kicked the guy's handgun off into the weeds by the side of the road and then kicked the asshole in the gut for good measure.

I pulled up the sleeve of Max's shirt just to be sure it was just a flesh wound and it was, but that was too close. Too fucking close. Kneeling down by the dick licker, I stared at him, my gun pointed to his head. "What the fuck is this about?"

The jackass grinned. "Payback's a bitch."

"That would be you, pussy. Are you going to make me ask you again or are we gonna be adults about this?"

"Fuck. You." He laughed and I joined in, realizing the absurdity of the moment while I was in it. I stuck my finger behind his ear, a move I learned in the military.

"Ow, you motherfucker! Goddamn piece of shit!"

"That pain you feel right now, that's my finger." He panted and squirmed but the pain was too intense for him to truly fight back. "But you see when I do that," I applied more pressure and his body sagged in relief. "The pain goes away but just imagine how it'll feel when I release that spot."

His eyes went wide, his breaths were even shallower. "Fuck, man! I don't know."

"That's not good enough." I let the pressure go and he howled in pain. "See? Now tell me why the fuck you're shooting at us."

"We don't know, okay? Boss man said—"

"Boss man, who? White Boy Craig?"

"No, Vigo sent us."

# HEAVENLY HACKED

I looked up and both Max and Savior were scowling. "To kill us?"

"No. To make a grab for whatever's in the van."

"Piece of shit!" Savior yelled at the kid, who I could see now was just that, a kid. Probably not even a full fucking club member yet. I stood and held Savior back. "What the fuck Jag, he just—"

"He just told us exactly what we needed to know." Vigo wasn't looking to kill us, not yet anyway. He wanted to make us do something stupid so the feds could step in and freeze our cash, maybe hand out a few promotions afterward. That wouldn't happen, not on my fucking watch. "Let's get out of here."

"And leave them? You fuckin' nuts, man?"

Yeah, I was nuts. I turned to the kid, still writhing on the ground. "Tell Rizzoli he better watch his fucking back!" We all walked away and took off down the road, eager to check on our Prez and our guns.

"What the hell was that?" Savior's voice was accusatory when we got back to the clubhouse. "We should've fucking killed those fuckers!" He got in my face like he always did, assuming because I wasn't always a loud mouth like him that I was a pushover.

"Some problems require you to use your brain man, not your fists." I could feel Cross's gaze on me, but I didn't turn to him. This was about Savior and him trusting that he wasn't the only guy in the room who could handle shit. "Vigo wants to test us, make us do something stupid but now we know he's still working with the feds."

"This kumbaya shit won't cut it, Jag."

I laughed. "Said the guy who was just bitching that a war with Roadkill might interfere with getting laid by his new girlfriend."

"Watch your mouth, mother fucker!" Savior yelled.

"Or what?" My chest puffed out, daring my brother to pick a fight with me.

## HEAVENLY HACKED

"Or I'll have to watch it for you." Savior was spoiling for a fight and that made me wonder what else was going on in his life.

"If you plan to watch my mouth, I better get some more lip balm." I smacked my lips together and Savior smiled.

"Asshole. We should have kicked his fuckin' ass!"

My lips parted in a smile. "You might just get your chance, man. Relax."

Easy for him to say when Mandy worked in one of the most secure locations in the whole damn city.

"I'm about to, Jag. Got a whole new shipment of guns to play with. Wanna come?"

"No can do, gotta go make sure Lasso and Vivi are still alive." They would be. I was sure of it.

I hoped.

## HEAVENLY HACKED

# Chapter Eighteen

*Vivi*

*You don't know who you're messing with.*

That was all the anonymous text message said. If it was meant to scare me, it failed spectacularly in pointing out the obvious. I didn't know, not yet, but I had a pretty good idea who it was. If scaring me was the goal, then I was being chased by the stupidest criminal on the planet.

"I have a pretty good idea," I said out loud as I deleted the message, but not before checking out the metadata to confirm it was routed through an anonymous third party carrier, which meant it couldn't be traced. Not without a court order.

The asshole had to be Blaise because Rizzoli had his plate full at the moment. The other asshole, Rizzoli, not the governor, had attacked Jag and his guys on their way back from wherever they'd gone. Though Jag didn't say it, the move had shaken all of them. Hell, it had shaken me too. Made me realize just how dangerous life could be with a motorcycle club in your orbit.

Too bad I had plans for Rizzoli. Plans to fuck up his whole world and then shit all over it. "That's entirely too much damn thinking before the alarm goes off." Jag's thick arms wrapped around my waist, his hot hands roaming the expanse of my skin until I shivered.

"How do you know how much thinking I'm doing?"

"The damn grinding gear shifts woke me up. What's on your mind?"

"Your friend was shot, Jag. That easily could have been you and I fucking hate it."

He turned me onto my back and leaned onto his torso so we were chest to chest, deep brown eyes smiling and serious as they seared through me. "I'm glad you hate it because it means you care but this is my life Vivi."

## HEAVENLY HACKED

I knew that, I'd been telling myself that since he picked me up from Lasso and Rocky's place. His life was constant danger and threats. It was something I needed to keep telling myself until it stuck. "I'm aware, Jag. Doesn't mean it's a pleasant experience. Anyway, I was just ... plotting."

His smile widened as his lips closed in on me, pressed against mine slow and sensual. "You're really sexy when you go all evil genius on me, you know that?"

"Tell me more," I purred and wrapped my arms around his neck. My legs followed suit as his hips pressed against mine, not enough to give me exactly what I wanted but just enough to send shards of light shooting out behind my eyes.

"I do more showing than talking," he said with a laugh, the blunt tip of his cock resting right at my opening, making me clench with desire. I spread my legs wider and Jag began to fill me magnificently. Beautifully. Spectacularly.

"Jeremiah, please." My back arched into him and his hands gripped my waist hard and pounded into me, fucking me to within an inch of my life. He thrust deep until I cried, until I moaned and called out his name like he was the only one who could save me. Who could keep me from flying off into the stratosphere as my orgasm crashed over me in thick, heavy waves that made me feel drugged. Like I was having an out of body experience. "Fuck me, Jag. That was…"

"Intense?"

"As fuck," I agreed as we both laughed in the sexually charged moment. I groaned when Jag's ringing cell phone began skipping across the nightstand beside him. "You're popular."

"It's an unknown number." He frowned at the screen and I could see the hesitation on his face.

"Answer it." I snatched the phone from his hand and pressed the talk button. And then the speakerphone.

"Yeah," he barked into the phone.

"You've gone too fucking far, nerd boy. I'll make sure you and your whole fucking club pays for this, asshole!" It was Vigo Rizzoli. I'd played the recording of his voice at least a hundred times before, so I was certain of that.

"I'm gonna need more details than that, Macaroni."

He growled into the phone. "My fucking money. You fucking stole all of my money and I know it was you. Give it back and this won't get ugly."

Jag held up a hand to stop the smartass remark poised to leap off my lips. "Money? Why on earth would I want a few thousand dollars when we have several profitable businesses?" He was doing his best to sound like some suburban poindexter, which only pissed Rizzoli off more.

"Don't fuck around with me Jag! I will end you and that bitch of yours. But first I'll let all my boys have a ride on that sweet pussy and then I'll put a bullet between her motherfuckin' eyes."

Jag clenched his jaws and fists as he listened to the vitriol coming from the phone and I knew he was angry. More than angry. "The same way your boys tried—and failed—to take out me and my crew? Glad to see you rodents are keeping your standards as low as ever."

"Put the money back, Jag." His voice was low and infused with steel to show he meant business. Jag only grinned at the phone.

"I don't know what the fuck you're talking about, Vigo but I wish I had stolen your chump change just so I'd be the one responsible for causing you this pain, but it wasn't me. Your sparkling personality must have pissed someone else off."

"Fucking liar! Get ready for war you piece of shit."

Jag reached for the phone, but I took three steps away from him. "If anything happens to Jag or any of his friends or any of their family, you will never see that money again. Test me and I'll take even more." I ended the call. "Talking to that greaseball makes me feel dirty. I feel like I need a shower now."

## HEAVENLY HACKED

He grinned and licked his full lips while I let my gaze slide down to the tent in the sheet over his lap. "Yeah, Vivi. Really fucking hot when you go all evil genius."

Normally I'd hate a nickname like that but coming from Jag it sounded kind of all right. "Yeah? You all hot and bothered, Jag?" Hands on my hips, I stood tall and took a step toward him. He nodded and beckoned me closer.

"Hell yeah, I am." He stroked his naked cock, already thick and hard and ready. And all for me. "But…you stole Vigo Rizzoli's money?"

"Not really. Right now it's just in a kind of limbo where it exists but doesn't. If I'm dead the money will stay where it is. Forever."

"Why?"

"I told you. I didn't like thinking about you getting hurt."

"So you wiped him out?"

"Not exactly. I left one account available to him and I really hope he decides to use it." Because it would be the beginning of the end for him and that day couldn't come soon enough for me. As soon as I could stop worrying about Vigo Rizzoli, I could put my focus back where it belonged.

On Governor Blaise.

\*\*\*

After spending the morning digging deep into any journalists and paparazzi who'd ever reported on Blaise, I'd learned a lot about Roger Stanhope Blaise in the past six hours. He was a hometown Florida boy who ignored his small town, working class background and married up to a Connecticut blue blood who loved the Florida sun. Unfortunately, the rumors of Roger's affinity for younger girls had plagued him since the early days of his political career. Well, *unfortunate* for him because I found it quite fortuitous.

## HEAVENLY HACKED

The one good thing about the paparazzi was that you could count on them to be as mercenary as possible. Cash was king and fortunately for both of us, I had plenty of it. And there was one guy, a real greaseball with a mullet and a penchant for acid wash jeans. Terry Murphy. He somehow got all the goods, which meant he was the man I needed to see.

That and he was totally old school. Kept his photos offline. All the way the fuck *offline*.

"I don't know why I let you talk me into this, Vivi." Jag sat in the driver's seat because, heaven forbid, a man actually ever placed his butt in the passenger seat. Even though it was my car, I relented. Driving wasn't all that fun and driving in Los Angeles was the worst fucking thing ever.

"Because you know I'm right. This Terry dude is cautious. Too cautious for someone who takes the same damn photos of twenty-five other guys every time he snaps an image." It didn't make sense unless he had more. "The few non-celeb images to his credit were of Blaise. It's a lead, Jag. The only one I've got."

He sighed and smacked the steering wheel. "Dammit, Vivi this guy could be crazy!"

"And you're coming with me. We're both armed and possess above average intelligence, I think we'll be all right."

Jag nodded and rested a hand on my thigh. "I have no doubt about that Vivi, but that doesn't mean we need to go in there guns blazing. And by we, I mean *you.*"

"I don't even have a gun, just my blade. I'm just going to ask him a few questions and offer him some money for his research."

"Money for research? Another fake identity. Are you sure you're not the spy, Vivi?" His mouth was set in a grim line but there was a spark of humor in his deep brown eyes.

"Believe me, I'm sure about that. But there was a time in my life when I had a stalker, only he had skills to rival my own." I hated talking about it because it was the only other time in my adult life that I felt helpless.

## HEAVENLY HACKED

Not in control. "You know those big hackathons where the government and private corporations go in search of the best hackers in the world and throw money at them?"

"I'm familiar," he said with a chuckle that made me smile.

"Well he was there too, apparently. I barely even remember him because I just wanted to get in, get some contacts and get gone. But he saw me and wanted me and from there it went pretty fucking crazy. Calls at all hours, deliveries of flowers and jewelry and even lingerie. Then the asshole hacked into my webcam. Thank God he didn't see anything. I'm not that stupid."

"What happened? Did you kill him?"

I flashed a proud smile and rolled my eyes. "Unfortunately I didn't, but I did have several seasoned IDs at my disposal and that helped keep me a step or two ahead."

"And what was this asshole's name?" His big hands wrapped around the steering wheel tight enough to break it.

"Charles or Chaz or something. I don't even think we were formally introduced, just some weirdo who was fixated on me."

"And what happened to him?"

"Let's just say that you shouldn't stalk people when you're embezzling from your clients." After all the drama it ended with a whimper and not a bang. Thank fuck. "But the IDs took a lot of time and I refuse to let them go to waste."

"Makes sense. Let me guess, you don't leave home without them?"

"*No*, home is usually where most bad shit goes down. Anyway it's behind me. Now tell me why you're still dangerously single Jag."

"Dangerously?"

"Considering how many women you're surrounded by, you'd have to actively try not to get involved. That equals dangerously single, okay maybe compulsively single. How's that?" I knew most guys weren't too eager to couple up and sleep with just one woman, but Jag seemed like the kind of guy made for a one-woman relationship.

"I guess I kind of am. Coupled up," he clarified without looking at me. The jerk. He knew exactly how his words sounded but refused to clarify until we'd gone about ten miles. "You're living with me and sleeping with me, plus we're on a road trip, which is basically a vacation. That's more serious than I've ever gotten with any woman."

His words shouldn't have made me feel such a sense of relief, but they did. "Me too," I admitted quietly, feeling uncertain at my own brief display of vulnerability. Since I was thirteen, I learned to keep my own counsel. If I didn't divulge my secrets and weaknesses to the world, they couldn't be used against me.

Ever.

We finally made it into Los Angeles and to the quiet West Hollywood neighborhood where Terry lived. "I should go up first. Alone."

Jag frowned and rejected the idea outright, just as I knew he would. "You really are fucking crazy if you think I'll let that happen."

I rolled my eyes. "You can't stop me, Jag. And you know he's more likely to open up to a woman." Men were simple creatures that way.

"Or he's going to grab you and pull you into his house, maybe keep you in his basement before burying you under the tomatoes."

I stared at him for a long moment and then burst out laughing. "That's an active imagination you have, Jag. The guy's a photographer, not a serial killer."

"They're not mutually exclusive Vivi. I'm coming with you," he said and then stepped from the car, leaving me ensconced in the dark while he walked around and opened the door for me. "Come on. I'll follow your lead." Jag pulled me out of the car and

## HEAVENLY HACKED

pressed me between him and the cool metal of the door, his lips closed in on mine. The kiss was slow and simmering. Just enough to make me want more. "Just keep your knife against that fine ass. Please."

"Fine." The walk up to Terry's little bungalow was nearly overgrown with a beautiful English garden that needed serious tending. "That's unexpected," I said as I rang the bell and waited. It was late afternoon so I took a chance he'd be home during the day. If not, I had a few leads.

The knob turned and someone disengaged several locks before the door opened. Slowly revealing a man with a longish red mullet and dark green eyes, freckles galore under his wife beater and acid wash jeans.

Acid. Wash. Jeans.

"Yeah, whadda ya want?" He was gruff and on the wrong side of grumpy, but this was too important.

"Hi Mr. Murphy, I'm Victoria Vivischenko and was hoping you could answer a few questions for me about some of your photos."

His eyes went wide in recognition. "Hell no. All my pics are clean and legal so fuck off!"

I held up my hands and kept up a polite smile. Men always felt at ease when you approached them with sugary sweetness. "I'm not a lawyer and I don't represent any celebrities. I was hoping you could tell me everything you know about Roger Blaise. Everything."

For a second I thought I had him, but Terry's sneer returned and he took a step forward. Jag had taken a step to match him but I waved my sweet protector off. Right now, getting info was far more important. "What's a sweet girl like you want to know about a scumbag like that for?" He leaned forward and flicked my hair from my shoulder.

I didn't like to be touched without permission and instinct kicked in. "Don't ever put your hands on me, asshole. Now, can you help me with this guy or not?"

Even with my blade pressed against the base of his throat, Terry didn't flinch and he didn't beg. What the crazy bastard did, was smile. "I like 'em crazy girl, come on in."

I looked back at Jag who only shrugged and motioned for me to follow Terry. "What the fuck," I mouthed.

"He likes 'em crazy," he whispered in my ear and stayed close as we entered.

"So what's got you interested in ol' Blaise? Got a young sister in the family way and naming him as the father?"

It was a curious statement but right in line with what I'd been able to dig up on my own. "Not exactly, but you're in the right area."

He nodded and went to the kitchen, returning a few minutes later with a few beers. "Well, Blaise has had an underage girlfriend since his first term as state senator, at least. They were always around, too. Babysitters until his kids outgrew them and then they were all types of things, young entrepreneurs with a cleaning or car wash service, apprentice chefs and once even a cheerleading coach. He's crafty about it, but not crafty enough."

He popped the top off of a beer and handed it to me. Then he handed one to Jag. I took the beer and nodded thanks as we sat on the dingy sofa. "Not to be rude but, how does a pap know all of this?"

He grinned and for a moment I could see beyond the mullet and jeans. "I wasn't always chasing celebs. I used to be an actual journalist at *The Herald* but my Blaise stories were squashed one too many times by the editor and we parted ways." Terry took a long pull from his beer and sighed. "This job pays better and more people give a shit about it."

It was a sad state of affairs, but it was absolutely fucking true. Politicians cheated on everyone from their kids and wives to their constituents, but no one cared as much when there were important stories out there, like which starlet stole which pop princess's boyfriend.

No fucking thanks.

## HEAVENLY HACKED

"Do you have anything else? I'm willing to pay you for your information, Terry."

He shook his head. "You seem to already know what kind of guy he is."

"Let's just say I found out some things I shouldn't have and he's not too pleased about it."

"Well I have some stuff," he said. He got up and rooted around in his desk before coming back to his seat. He gave me a long look as if confirming something about me in his mind and then slid a flash drive to me. "Think about this; he's governor with no good excuse to have underage girls surrounding him. How is he getting his fix?"

I had a feeling Terry had the answer. I took a pull from my beer while Jag sat silently beside me and got comfortable. Whatever Terry was willing to share, I needed to hear.

And we had all the time in the world to listen to him.

# Chapter Nineteen

*Jag*

"You wanna tell me why the fuck a bunch of our prospects were attacked at Shandy's?" I opened the door to find three pissed off bikers, Cross, Gunnar and Savior, darkening my doorstep.

"How in the fuck should I know?" I stepped back to let the guys enter now that I knew what in the hell they were doing on my doorstep at eleven at night. Without a fucking call.

"How about because that asshole Rizzoli is claiming you stole from him," Cross spat at me. "Tell me you didn't."

His words sent a white-hot rage pulsing through me. "If you have to ask then it doesn't matter what the fuck I have to say, does it?" I led them into the kitchen and took up the spot against my fridge. Waiting. Angry and waiting.

"Come on, man just tell us. You and Blue Hair planning on taking the Roadkill cash and blowing out of town?" Gunnar leaned back and put his big fucking boots on my table.

"Get your fucking feet off my table." I wasn't in the mood for bullshit, particularly Gunnar's brand of bullshit. "Is there anything else you need to accuse me of or are you ready to get the fuck out?"

"We had to ask, Jag." Savior, attempting to be the voice of reason, was laughable.

"You really didn't but I guess it's good to know where I stand." I would never fucking tell the guys but hearing them say that shit, hurt. I never once, not since I became a Reckless Bastard, felt like an outcast or an outsider. No one gave a damn that I was black or that I was the only black member. But right now, I felt like an outsider and it had nothing at all to do with the color of my skin. "We done?"

"You gonna act like a pussy now?" Gunnar stood.

## HEAVENLY HACKED

"Pussy? Fuck you, Gunnar. You vanish for more than a year and come back with a chip on your shoulder acting like an asshole and the rest of us put up with it because you have a kid to deal with. Well so fucking what and fuck you too!"

"And the money?" Cross's voice was deadly quiet.

"I told you I didn't fucking take it but I guess Vigo's words carry more weight than mine. Fine, believe what the fuck you want. Just get the fuck out. Now."

"Jag be reasonable," Savior tried again.

"Reasonable? Is it reasonable to come to my motherfuckin' house and accuse me based on the word of a man who wants us dead? Burned our fucking plants just to get the feds off his back?" I glared at Savior. "Yeah, I didn't fucking think so."

"So who took the fucking money?"

"I did." Vivi stood in the doorway of the kitchen wearing a hell of a lot more clothes than she had on when I left the bedroom.

"Why?"

She shrugged. "Why shouldn't I? I'm not part of your little biker club and I don't answer to any of you. I do what I need to do for me." She smacked her chest with the palm of her hand to drive the point home and damn, that chick really did have a piece of me. She was tough as hell, took no shit from anyone and didn't back down from a fight she could win.

"No matter who it hurts?" Gunnar stared at her, his eyes angry and full of fire and accusation.

"You deal with your shit and I'll deal with mine."

"*Your* shit seems to be causing problems with *our* shit," Cross reminded her.

Vivi laughed. "Bull*shit*. When I pulled up you were knee-deep in *shit*. Cops, guns, helicopters and ambulances. Seems like you had problems with them *before* I showed up. As a matter of fact if it wasn't for me and *my shit* you wouldn't know that it was your little friend who burned your fucking plants, would you?" She didn't wait for an answer. "Exactly, so maybe you should take a fucking chill pill. I took his money and I'm not giving it back until I'm good and fucking ready. When I know I'm safe and don't need to control that piece of shit, I might give it back." She leaned against the wall and glared at each man, including me. "Or maybe I'll just take the cash and blow out of town."

Cross took a step forward and Vivi took a step back, hand sliding to her back pocket and I knew the shit would hit the fan in a minute.

"Put. The. Money. Back."

She shot me a look, those grey eyes boring into me. "Jag, you need to calm your boy here. And as long as I have it, I might make it out of this shitty town alive."

"No. Fuck *that*," Savior piped in. "These assholes won't stop until they have their money and now we're caught up in *your* bullshit."

Vivi laughed. "You want the money? Then go fucking get it." She turned and left the kitchen but instead of heading back upstairs, she slammed the front door, which meant I was sleeping alone tonight.

A big ass sigh escaped because I was tired. Dog fucking tired of always fighting, always going. Always fucking *on*. It hadn't stopped over the past year and I was just beat. Whether they realized it or not, all three of my brothers had just made everything more difficult than it needed to be. "Happy?"

"She can't keep that money, Jag." Cross's words were insistent and bordered on an order, but I only stared. "You know that."

"What I know is that I spent the whole fucking trip back from LA trying to convince of her that and thanks to your so-called help, Vivi is going to do exactly what the fuck she wants. When she wants."

"Naw, man. That ain't good enough, brother." Gunnar smacked his hands together and went to the fridge, grabbing a beer.

"Now we're brothers? Five minutes ago I was a fuckin' thief."

## HEAVENLY HACKED

"You on your period, Jag?"

"Fuck you, Gunnar. Shouldn't you be babysitting?" He flipped me off but I'd already turned back to Cross. "I didn't know about the money until Rizzoli called, pissed as fuck. But I won't ask her to give it back until I can be sure Roadkill won't fuck with her."

"That's if she's telling the truth and from where I'm sitting that's a big fucking if," Savior said, following Gunnar to pull a beer from the fridge.

"You didn't believe Mandy either until she took a beatdown in the parking lot of her job. Maybe you should try learning from your mistakes."

He growled, pissed that I'd brought it up but I was beyond caring. "Is that how this club works now? We have to make sure Savior believes someone before we take care of it?"

Cross sighed and dropped down into one of the kitchen chairs. "Jag we're in a bad position here."

"Don't you think I fuckin' know that? If you don't want any part of this, fine. But I won't abandon Vivi.

And even if she isn't around, Roadkill is still a problem. You fucking saw what Rizzoli did, but you took his word over mine, anyway." I was so fucking done. I wanted to walk away but we had more shit to discuss. "That's not all."

"Did you also get married while you were in La-La Land?" Savior asked me and took a seat at the end of the table.

"Fuck you, Savior." I replied, and the son of a bitch laughed. "It's about Blaise. The guy is a fucking scumbag."

"Says Vivi?"

"No Gunnar, says *me*. Asshole." I didn't know what his problem was, but I was past giving a shit. "We went to see a guy who used to be a journalist ... until he tried to run one too many stories about Blaise and his penchant for underage pussy."

"And?"

"And Vivi is working on a plan to get him to stop. I just need to know if I can count on the club for help or not." The room fell silent except for the sounds of four angry bikers breathing heavily.

"*Vivi* is working on a plan? She gonna steal from him too?"

"Since he's tried to kill her at least three goddamn times, I'd say she's in her rights if that's what she chooses. What the fuck would you do if it were Maisie?"

"But it's not," he barked at me, pounding the table with his meaty fist.

"But it could be. Vivi is the victim here in case you fucking forgot. Either Blaise or Rizzoli want her dead because of what she's seen, do you fucking get that? She's seen some deep dark secrets about these assholes and I happen to be worried about her." I stood. "You know what? I don't give a shit. Get the fuck out," I told them and left the kitchen, heading upstairs to my empty fucking bedroom.

There were so many thoughts going through my mind but not one of them could catch hold to become a fully formed idea. I couldn't fucking believe it; my club didn't have my back. After all the shit we'd been through together and this was where they chose to draw the line.

*Vivi* was where they drew the line.

Un-fucking-believable.

***

"I can't believe they're acting like this!" And now I was acting like a whiny little bitch in front of my woman and that didn't feel good at all.

"Fuck 'em, Jag. I mean the whole point of all that shit is that you have each other's backs, right?" She didn't even wait for a response. "Think of all the shit you've done for them, shit that could put you in prison. All that and they can't get over their hate of me?"

"They don't hate you," I said automatically.

"Don't kid yourself, Jeremiah. They hate me and that's okay. I don't really give a shit. But I care that they're doing this to you." She fidgeted with the hem of her black t-shirt and her eyes darted around the room, uncomfortable with any display of emotion. I loved that about her.

"They don't. Hell, Lasso even likes you. It's just that they're worried. We've had a lot of problems with people lately and most of them have had to do with the women in our lives." I told her about Teddy's stalker who happened to be one of the Reckless Bitches and about Mandy's problem with Roadkill thanks to a so-called friend. "And you already know Rocky's story."

She whistled and then smiled. "Well that's what happens when you're in a biker gang, Jag."

"Motorcycle club," I corrected even though I knew she only did that to get under my skin.

"Right," she said and rolled her eyes playfully. "It's getting late and I've worked hard all day. I think it's time for a treat."

I loved it when Vivi turned playful and I loved it more when she ripped her shirt off to reveal her delicious tits. They were round and perky with perfect pink nipples. Perfectly *hard* pink nipples. "I do love a tasty treat," I told her and when she turned and headed up the stairs, I followed her.

And caught her on the stairs, making her laugh. "Tasty?"

"You know damn well you are," I told her and spun her around, kissing the hell out of her right there on the stairs. Her lips were soft and pliant, moving with mine as I led the dance. One leg wrapped around my thigh so my hips sank against hers and she moaned, tilting her head back so I could taste her beautiful neck. She arched into me. I fucking loved it when she did that.

"Jag." The way she sighed my name sent a rod of heat straight to my cock, which I pressed into her. Hard.

"Vivi. Babe." The way she opened her legs a little more when she sighed told me exactly what she wanted. I snapped the button on her jeans and slid my hand inside until the wet warmth of her pussy touched my fingertips. "Damn you're so wet already. For me?"

She nodded, mouth open slightly inviting me in for another taste. I devoured her mouth this time while two fingers slid deep into her tight pussy. She was so fucking wet, so tight, she clenched around me and I knew she was already close. "Yes." Her hips circled into me and one hand clamped the back of my neck, her teeth sank into my lips.

"Someone's feeling greedy."

"Damn right, ah!" She sucked in a breath when my thumb found her clit and her other hand grabbed my wrist. "Jag!"

She was so close, and my fingers began to thrust deeper and faster, the only sound was her sexy fucking gasps she made when her orgasm was close. Her pussy clenched hard, the warning before the storm.

Just before she came, a loud explosion sounded outside. Close as fuck outside, like on my damn property. Unfortunately that sound and the fiery light that lit up the entire front of the house made Vivi's orgasm a distant memory.

"Fuck! What the fuck was that, a bomb?"

I was already headed to the front window, the one in the corner with the table that held one of my guns. I pushed the curtain aside and saw two guys running away. "Close, a fucking explosion!"

I was out the door in seconds, grabbing another gun before I aimed at one of the fuckers running away. Lining up my shot, I got the fucker and he fell down.

"Shit! Go!" a man moaned.

I recognized the voice but with all the noise and chaos I couldn't place it. Not that it mattered. I unloaded my clip into the mother fucker.

"Shit!" Vivi said beside me, staring at the wreckage. "Holy fuck is that...?"

"The Crown Vic from the tow company? Yeah." It was there in the middle of my fucking yard. On fire. "Those sirens are definitely headed here so we need to put what we need into your camper—"

## HEAVENLY HACKED

"And get it off this fucking property." She was already heading back into the house to get who knew what while I went to the guy lying still on the ground.

He didn't look familiar but that didn't mean shit. He could be a hired gun, or he could be a Roadkill rookie, well he could have been. Now he was just a body. Food for worms.

"Get his ID," Vivi shouted from behind the wheel of her camper. "So we can figure out who the hell sent him! Now!"

I reached into his front pockets and there was nothing. "Back pockets are empty too!"

"Shit." With a muttered curse, Vivi parked her camper at the end of the road and ran back, the sound of sirens growing louder with every passing second. "Did you look in his shoe?"

I looked at her over my shoulder. "Seriously, who in the hell are you girl?"

She grinned. "I am an enigma wrapped in a little mystery, chaos and charm and then rolled up in a pretty little hacker package."

That much was true and she turned out to be right about the ID. "When this is all over Vivi, we're going to have a serious talk." I handed her the ID and she slid it into her own shoe.

"Maybe." Finally the lights and sirens were on us. "Remember don't say more than you need to." She turned serious gray eyes my way until I nodded.

"This isn't my first rodeo, Vivi."

She shrugged. "I have to be sure, considering how clueless you were about the ID in the shoe thing." Her smile took the sting off the words and seconds later we were inundated with police.

"Yeah well, just make sure you don't give them the wrong ID."

She frowned. "I'm not giving them shit."

"That's my girl." I pressed a quick, hard kiss to her lips as two officers approached with firefighters and

## HEAVENLY HACKED

ambulances behind them. There was a big shit show in my front yard and I knew it would be hours before we were alone again. Especially with the dead guy in the yard. That wouldn't go over well with the cops.

Turns out, it took even longer than I'd thought. But the self-defense story worked, and the cops told us not to leave town. Not that we would. I had a feeling this was the start of a bigger war with Roadkill—or the feds. Whoever the dead guy belonged to.

The first streaks of sun lit the sky before the last vehicle pulled away, with the crispy Crown Vic in tow. "Now where can we park this thing and get some sleep?"

"Sleep? I thought for sure you'd want another crack at that interrupted orgasm." I hoped she did because I sure as fuck needed to relax after the night we'd had.

"Who said I don't? I just need to recharge my batteries and wash the fire stank off me."

"Come on, I know a place." If the guys were still full of bullshit, I knew Lasso would let us stay at his place. But, I didn't want to put him and Rocky in danger, so we made our way to the clubhouse first.

# Chapter Twenty

*Vivi*

"Where in the hell have you been? I've been going out of my damn mind!" Jag was so adorable when he got all worried mother hen on me. No one had ever fussed over me before and even though it was *kind of* annoying, it was outweighed by just how sweet it was.

"I was out. Rocky told me all about Mandy's new chocolate shop and I thought I'd check it out." And I had. For about five minutes before taking a long, wandering circuitous route around the Siren Casino and Resort. The places looked exactly like the plans, which was foolish considering just how much cash a casino had on hand. Security or not, with the layout of the whole resort, a smart criminal could win big. "What's up?"

"What's up is that I've been calling you all afternoon and you weren't answering. I thought something had happened."

Dammit this man knew how to warm my cold black heart. "I'm sorry I worried you. I brought you some chocolate."

He winced and then laughed. "Okay." I licked my lips and gave him a dark look.

He tossed a crooked smile at me. "But you already taste so sweet."

I batted my eyelashes and pulled the camper door shut behind me. "Everything was fine. I took every precaution and I made sure I wasn't followed."

"Good. You ready to tell me what you're up to next?"

"Not yet."

"Then when?" He stood when I did and pushed into my space. "I'm here to help you. I might try to talk you out of something crazy stupid but if you're set on it, you know I got your back." One hand cupped my face and God help me, but I leaned into it. Let the warmth of his palm sink into my body. It felt good. Really fucking good and I didn't want to talk about the fight for my life that was on the horizon. Right now I just wanted one thing.

"Damn. Jag. I need you."

His grin was dark and sexy, and filled with promise. "Yeah?"

"Oh yeah." I grabbed a fistful of his shirt and crashed our mouths together, fusing them in a kiss so hot and fiery that there was no way we'd ever part. Instead of scaring me, the thought thrilled me. Inspired me. "Now, Jeremiah. I need you now."

This kiss was different than the others; there was no teasing and no joking smiles. It was just me and him. Jag and Vivi. Jeremiah and Genevieve. Raw need and wild hunger. It was the realest kiss I'd ever shared with a man and I didn't want it to end.

"Not yet," he said, throwing my words back in my face.

I laughed and slid my hands under his shirt, scraped my nails up his rock-hard abs and his tight pecs. He really was a beautiful man and he was wearing too many damn clothes. "Now," I told him and pushed the shirt over his head, hungry as hell to get close to him. Closer. So fucking close I didn't know where I ended and he began.

Jag growled and tore the t-shirt from my body, chest heaving as he stared hungrily at my tits.

"Fuck, you're so beautiful. And braless."

His big calloused hands cupped my ass and lifted me onto the dinette table.

"And wearing too many fucking clothes," he growled and in seconds had remedied the problem. "Better." He dipped low, sucking slow at first and then harder until I pushed into him and my nipple disappeared into his mouth. I couldn't look away, not from the sight of his thick plump lips doing wicked things to my body.

"Jag," I moaned, making all sorts of noises as he moved back and forth, pleasing and torturing me. "No more. I can't wait." My hands fumbled with his belt and jeans until he shoved them aside and did what I could not. "Thank fuck."

He chuckled, staring at me while he fisted his cock, stroking in long hard strokes. "You ready?"

I spread my legs wider until I nearly straddled the table. "See for yourself." Jag wasn't playing around today. He didn't dive right in, instead he took two fingers and rubbed them up and down my pussy, making sure I was completely coated in my own juices before he dropped down to his knees.

"Stay just like that," he growled. The order was issued in a deep, commanding voice that forced obedience. And fucking hell, was that obedience returned ten-fold. His mouth worked me over. Kissing my pussy like a teenager in the back seat for the first time, the kiss was endless. My body shook and trembled beneath the swirl of his tongue, the way his hands branded my thighs as he held them apart.

His tongue touched my clit and that was it. My hips bucked off the table so eager to get close to the source of all that heat and all that pleasure.

"Jag."

His name was the only word my brain could find, and it seemed to fire him up, which was just hot to watch.

He stood and stroked my pussy with his thumb. "Vivi," he whispered, barely able to speak and stepped closer until his thick cock was at my opening and he pushed in deep in one long slide.

"Oh, fuck!" he moaned as if he were in pain, the kind of pain that meant endless pleasure.

But that was the end of the slowness. There was no more teasing or playing, Jag was in full pleasure seeking mode as he fucked me. Hard and fast and dirty. He cupped my face and my legs wrapped around his waist, giving him just enough room to pound into me deliciously hard. Each time his balls smacked me, a shiver ripped through me.

"Vivi," he growled again, gaze locked on mine. The intensity of it stole my breath.

# HEAVENLY HACKED

I leaned back on the table and that only deepened his reach. So hard and thick, he filled up all the free space and I loved it. Rolling my hips and urging him on, I needed it all. "Yes, Jag. Oh, fuck yeah!"

"You feel amazing."

"You feel better," I told him back and squeezed.

"Ah, fuck." He reared up and palmed my tits, kneading and pinching my nipples while he fucked me hard and fast. It was too much, and I was feeling so much pleasure as my body began to overheat. The passion swirled around the room, crackling in the air between us like it was a second away from combusting.

My orgasm started at my toes, making my legs numb as it crawled up my body, but when the heat reached my pussy, all was lost. Pleasure swamped me, filled me with a heat as bright and hot as the sun. My body shook and shivered and then convulsed violently as I rode out my ecstasy on his thick, dark cock while Jag still sought his own.

"Oh, Jag," I cried out and he grinned.

"I fucking love the way you say my name, babe." His hands crawled up my thighs and his thumb stopped at my clit. "But I need to feel you come again while I fill you up. Come for me again, Vivi. All over my cock."

His words were just dirty enough to get me going again or maybe it was his talented thumb rubbing a tornado over my clit until I shot off one more time. The deep strokes came faster and faster and then he was roaring my name and filling me with his come.

"Ah, Vivi! Fuck, Vivi!" He collapsed on top of me, panting. His big hard body felt good against mine, especially the way his cock twitched inside of me.

"That was amazing."

"Yes, you are."

We dozed off curled around each other, stars still swirling behind my eyes.

I was a coward, keeping my plan away from him until it was finalized. I trusted Jag, really, I did but I

## HEAVENLY HACKED

knew he would try to talk me out of it. The thing was, I was deathly afraid he just might do it.

***

Today was the day Governor Blaise arrived in Las Vegas for his big shit political fundraiser. He'd arrived with a small contingent of staffers, including his chief of staff, junior press secretary and his sixteen-year-old sidepiece masquerading as a twenty-two-year-old staffer, Sabrina. Not to mention three bodyguards, which his wife always insisted on thanks to her family's wealth.

Armed with the information I got from Terry, combined with my own not-above-board research, I was ready to go head to head with this dirtbag. I sprawled out on Jag's sofa watching Blaise and his crew smile for the cameras as the handsome and slimy owner of Siren Casino and Resort, Drake Foster greeted him, sharing Governor Dirt Bag's big, shit-eating grin. From one scumbag to another.

"Enjoy it while it lasts, motherfucker," I chucked at my computer screen.

Everything was all set. Friday was two days away, plenty of time to check and double check every phase of my plan. Then when Friday rolled around, I would do what I had to, and I'd leave Las Vegas for good. I didn't want to leave, not really. Jag was incredible, even more than I dreamed back when we talked every single day. He wasn't just a hot body and a good hacker; he was a good man. The best man. Kind and sweet, handsome and smart. He was damn near perfect.

He had a family. The Reckless Bastards were his tribe and they, for the most part, hated my fucking guts. So I would do what I came here to do and help Jag's club in the process. Then I would leave. I had no plan and no clue where I would go next. New York was ruined for me and I'd already put my apartment on the market. I was done with the east coast and thanks to Jag and his crew, I couldn't be on the west coast either.

## HEAVENLY HACKED

Maybe I'd move to Big Sky country. I'd heard Wyoming was beautiful in the springtime.

"You finally ready to talk?" Jag stood in the doorway between the living room and the kitchen looking delicious in nothing but a pair of burgundy boxers that hugged his thighs and his thick, semi-hard cock.

I wasn't ready to give him all the details, but he caught me off guard and distracted me with his beautiful body. "No, but a promise is a promise. I'm going to out Blaise." I braced myself for his response because I knew he wouldn't like it.

His posture proved it. Arms crossed and a disapproving scowl on his face. "Vivi you can't. Those girls are underage."

Question answered. "And that's why I'm going to out him. He's breaking the law, Jag, and that means it's going to come out one way or the other. At least if I leak it then I can be sure the media will cover it."

I closed down my laptop, sick of seeing Blaise's face smiling on every goddamn channel. "Oh, and it might save my life if that matters to you at all." Why was I being so bitchy to him? I didn't know but I had a feeling and I didn't want to examine it too closely.

"That's not fair, you know I care. But are you even thinking of the girls?"

I scoffed, disgusted at his view. "Oh please, these girls knowingly fucked a married man. I'm sorry Jag, but I'm not risking my life for young girls with daddy issues. Or an old fucking pervert. You know he's using his political power to screw these girls over." He sucked in a breath like one of the girls was his long-lost family and I knew this was going to be a problem.

"That's cold, Vivi. Even for you."

"It's a good thing I didn't ask for your opinion, isn't it?" It was also a good thing I'd already decided to leave Vegas or else I'd be really upset right about now.

"There's no other way?"

# HEAVENLY HACKED

I shook my head. "I looked, Jag, but going to the cops with the proof only helps if they do something about it. What if he's got the cops in his pocket? No one will do anything. The only way to make sure he's caught with his pants down is to make certain enough people know about his proclivities."

He gave me a disappointed look I'd been seeing on people's faces who were supposed to care about me—my parents, social workers and even that one foster family before I ran away—my entire life. I hated that look. It pissed me off because I didn't need anyone else to be disappointed in me. I did a good enough job of that all on my own.

"Vivi, think about it. Please."

"I have thought about it. Day after day after day. And something needs to be done about it. He's a freakin pervert!"

There was nothing more to say, not about this. He'd made his opinion clear and I disagreed. We were at an impasse.

Luckily it would be over on Friday, one way or the other.

# Chapter Twenty-One

*Jag*

Vivi was so goddamn stubborn. The woman could make the Pope lose his cool and I was far from his fucking holiness. I couldn't believe she refused to listen to reason where those girls were concerned. They were kids for fuck's sake and not in control of their actions.

"How could a woman have such a callous attitude towards little girls? Can you believe it?"

Lasso and Rocky stared at each other and then at me, their heads nodding in agreement.

"Jag, it's illegal. Those girls might have been all over Blaise, saying yes, yes, yes. Doesn't matter. If they are underage, there's no consent. Even if he didn't coerce them. Read the law," Rocky said, leaning forward and looking at me like maybe I didn't understand the English language. "It's no different than if that fifteen-year-old was dating a nineteen-year-old. Statutory rape. Hella illegal."

Lasso put a hand to his wife's shoulder to calm her down. "Did Vivi find any evidence he coerced the girls?"

"No. The opposite." She found emails and love letters, explicit images of Blaise and his girl of the moment along with explicit text messages. "They wanted to be with him," I admitted reluctantly. "But it doesn't make them *not* victims. He's a powerful man with a shit load of money. I think it's called abuse of power or something."

"So what you're saying is that she should protect *their* illegal secret at the risk of her *own* life? Don't be stupid," Rocky said in an unusually blunt way. "Maybe he promised them things if they sucked his dick. Sick bastard."

"Am I really being that stupid?"

"Yes. As a former teenage girl myself, I can tell you that I rarely dated a guy my own age. Even *he who shall*

## HEAVENLY HACKED

*never be named again* was eight years older than me." Ever since shit had gone down with her ex, Rocky refused to even mention the fucker's name. It made me love her even more for my brother.

I had a feeling that I was being worse than stupid. I was being ignorant. "Shit." My stupidity could've cost Vivi. Big. "I guess it's a good thing she basically told me to fuck off."

Rocky laughed, and Lasso shook his head, looking happier than I'd ever seen the guy. "She's definitely a firecracker," she agreed and rubbed her swollen belly.

The phone rang, and I picked it up automatically because shit had been so tense for such a long time that every ring could be an emergency. "Yeah?"

"Get to the clubhouse. Now."

I ended the call. "That was Cross. Something's up at the clubhouse." Those were the only words either of us needed to hear to be on our feet and headed toward the door. Bikes revving, chrome glinting under the late afternoon sun and fifteen minutes later we were pulling up to the clubhouse.

Everyone was outside, the guys and their girls plus a few Reckless Bitches. But what surprised me when Lasso and I drew closer was that there were half a dozen Roadkill MC members standing around with their chests puffed out. Looking like they were ready to start some shit.

Lasso strolled into the center of the group "What's going on?" He stood with his hands on his hips and a wide grin on his face. "Are the Roadkill boys here asking for coats for winter again," he joked.

A few Reckless Bastards laughed a little too hard, drawing glares from Roadkill. Their President, White Boy Craig, glared hard as he approached trying to intimidate a big fucker like Lasso who wasn't intimidated by anyone. "Real fucking funny cowboy. We don't need shit from you or your club."

Lasso grinned. "Then what the fuck are you doing here, reserving time for a fucking tea party?"

## HEAVENLY HACKED

"You think you're real fucking funny, don't you? How about I knock that smile off your face."

"How about you try it, dick breath?" Lasso stood taller, giving his five-inch-height difference more of an impact. "Or maybe you're just trying to get close to me since you're clearly missing your cellmate."

White Boy Craig laughed in a maniacal way that often happened before someone snapped but Lasso wasn't concerned. "Fuck you, Lasso."

"See boys, he wants a taste of me. Is that why you and your pussies are here? Because we ain't interested."

Craig snarled. "You know why we're here. The money. Rizzoli told us you took it."

Lasso laughed. "And you believe that songbird?" He looked to Cross and pointed to White Boy Craig. "Can you believe this shit?" Craig pushed Lasso when his back was turned but the big country fucker smiled and turned, slamming his fist against Craig's cheek with a deadly crack. "I ain't one of your prison bitches. Touch me again and I will fucking end you."

Two Roadkill members got in Lasso's face and the crazy bastard smiled. "Looks like my dance card is fillin' up here!" He head butted one guy and knocked the other out cold with one fucking punch. That started the shit right up. Fists flew from all directions before the dumb shit Roadkill assholes realized they were on our home fucking turf.

"You're outnumbered," I told White Boy Craig. "Stop this shit now before you end up dead."

"Is that a threat, *punk*?"

I smiled and got in his face. Guys like him always thought they could bait me by calling me names. "It's a promise, asshole. Look around. There are four of us, at least for every one of you. Stick around any longer and we'll be cleaning your blood and brains out of the asphalt until next summer."

"Do that and the rest of my organization will rain hell down on this shitty MC." For all his bravado,

## HEAVENLY HACKED

Craig's words were spoken with less fire because the asshole knew he was only alive because we allowed him to live.

Cross barked out a laugh. "How in hell can we be scared of a guy who doesn't even know what his own VP is doing behind his back?" Oh, shit. Cross was intending to use Vivi's info now, either to scare Craig or just to fuck with him.

"You're talking out your ass, Cross. My men are solid." He pounded a fist against his chest and his crew did the same. Jackasses. "If you had the proof you'd present it."

Yeah, Craig had a point. I pulled out my phone and texted Vivi. We hadn't talked much over the past couple of days since our argument, but I knew she wouldn't punish the whole club because we were having a disagreement. When a full minute passed without a response I began to worry. Maybe I didn't know Vivi the way I thought I did. Thoughts raced around my mind and every second she didn't respond worried me.

Was she ignoring me? Or had something happened to her?

Vivi might have been a little crazy, but she was trustworthy. Four long minutes later White Boy Craig's phone chimed and then the rest of them. He frowned at the phone, flipping through pages of shit that had me wondering just what Vivi had sent.

"This is for real? Vigo's workin' with the fuckin' Feds?"

Cross nodded, his expression more solemn because more than any of the rest of us, he knew exactly what Craig was feeling now.

Cross said cool as ice, "You need the fucking emails too?"

"Naw, I got 'em," he snarled and held up his phone. "Fuck, bank records too?"

It was the first I heard of them and that made me wonder what Vivi had done.

"You're welcome." Cross stood with his arms folded over his chest, a stoic expression on his face. He

## HEAVENLY HACKED

wasn't offering a kindness to Craig, just giving him the information to prove what kind of leader he was. If Vigo made it out of this alive, we would decimate Roadkill MC in less than a year. If he did what he needed to do, White Boy Craig might live long enough to turn his shitty club around.

Craig spit out, "This isn't over."

Cross answered, "You're goddamn right it ain't over. You assholes torched our weed and fucked up our whorehouse. When you get your house in order White Boy, we'll be ready for you. For now, get the fuck off my property."

We all stood and watched Roadkill MC hurry to their bikes, eager to get away from us but probably more eager to confront Vigo. Cross walked over to me and clapped me on the back. "Your girl came through for us."

I didn't bother telling him that she hadn't done a goddamn thing for the club.

"Yeah," was all I said in response. I needed to see Vivi. She was the only one I wanted to see right now.

"I'm serious. Did you see that shit she sent? Not only did she drain all the accounts but one, she also made it look like he was getting regular payments from the FBI."

Cross flashed a shit eating grin, so proud of some shit he had nothing to do with.

"He probably was," I said, trying to keep my attitude in check.

"She's all right," Gunnar agreed. And as every one of my brothers nodded with wide, shit eating grins, I felt nothing but disgust. "Yeah, well it would've been nice if you fuckers could have seen that before she saved your asses."

My gaze connected with Lasso, who flashed a sympathetic smile and nodded for me to go get my girl.

I couldn't fucking wait.

Only when I got to the camper, Vivi wasn't there.

HEAVENLY HACKED

# Chapter Twenty-Two

*Vivi*

I woke up early Friday morning mostly because I'd barely slept one fucking wink. Anxiety bubbled up in my belly all night making it hard to close my eyes, never mind to sleep. My mind raced with all the possibilities of what could go wrong. Foremost was that no one would believe it. Blaise and his followers had an impressive knack for ignoring facts that didn't fit their preconceived beliefs.

Luckily for me there would be just enough press at the event to matter.

Hopefully.

I took a quick shower, careful not to disturb Jag, although I was pretty sure he'd been awake for at least an hour based on his breathing. Either way he was giving me my space and I appreciated it. I didn't want to spend my last few hours with Jag fighting and neither did he, so he didn't ask me about my plans and I didn't offer up anything.

I tugged a blonde wig styled into a bob over my head, tucking in all the loose ends and popped in non-prescription blue contacts. A last glance in the mirror before I snuck out assured me I looked like a completely different person. Off to meet my accomplice.

"Damn girl, you look *muy caliente!*" Rocky was a crazy ass chick who I would be sad to say goodbye to, which would be just a few minutes after she helped me get ready for the big overpriced political ass-kissing contest.

"How are you so chipper this time of morning? I asked, my eyes popping at her cheery smile. "It's unnatural."

She rubbed her belly, skin glowing like it was radioactive. "Morning? Is it morning? This little bugger has been doing backflips and half-time routines on my bladder since midnight. This is noon for me, which is why we're stopping to grab some lunch."

## HEAVENLY HACKED

Luckily this town never slept, not ever, which meant we could get anything from sushi to hamburgers or tacos any time. Day or night. "Wouldn't that technically be breakfast?"

"Ugh, fine. Brunch, then." Rocky had a bit of a lead foot, so I kept a tight grip on the 'oh shit' bar as she rolled through a drive thru and placed her order. "You want anything?"

I frowned at her. "That's not for me, too?" My lips twitched and when her mouth turned down into a frown, I cracked. "No, I'm good. Too nervous to eat."

"You'll be fine," she said, handing me the bag of food while she took us back to her place. Lasso was still sleeping when we arrived, and we snuck into one of the guest rooms.

"I've got everything all set," she assured me. "I went to the hotel boutiques and got three different outfits, all perfect for a fair skinned...blonde?"

"Yes, going with blonde today."

Rocky made quick work of two breakfast burgers, taking a break to look up at me in the second outfit, an emerald green shirt dress. "That looks great...but maybe a little too great. You look kind of hot."

"Okay." I picked up the final outfit, a hot pink dress with a matching jacket. "This style will probably be worn by half the women in attendance, with some variety." I stood with my hands on my hips as Rocky looked me over.

"You still look hot, but I think you're right. At least fifty women will be wearing something like this. Just, maybe hunch your shoulders a little."

"I look ridiculous but once you do my makeup I'll totally look the part." I hoped. I bought a legitimate ticket under an alias just so I could be there when that motherfucker saw everything he worked for fall apart. Not in front of the world, because despite what Jag thought of me, I would never do that to teenage girls. Not even ones who went after married dudes. No, this would be a controlled explosion. One that would only detonate in front of the people who mattered most to

# HEAVENLY HACKED

him. Who held his career in their hands and wouldn't hesitate to crush him before he brought the whole party down.

Rocky painted some pink gloss on my lips as a nice finishing touch. "Are you sure you wanna do this?"

I nodded. "I don't want to—I have to. Thank you so much for this, Rocky. And remember, ninety minutes and then you can tell Jag." I pulled her in for a hug and rubbed her belly for good luck before leaving.

I walked a few blocks and grabbed a taxi to the resort. There was still plenty of time before the fundraiser started and I didn't want to draw any attention to myself. I needed to blend in.

After exchanging a few hundred bucks in chips, I hit the blackjack table, winning and losing at equal parts in an effort not to draw attention. I hit a few more tables and some slot machines before it was time for me to follow the herd to the ballroom for the high-priced, fund-raiser lunch.

Table nine was where they placed Amanda Schwartz, so I made my way there and looked around at my tablemates. I guessed mid-level political types happy to rub elbows with the party elite. I took a seat and sipped water from a crystal glass, smiling politely at the silver hairs and good ol' boys hoping to get ahead this weekend.

The chicken was dry, and the green beans were undercooked, but the one glass of champagne I had was nice and cold. Just how I liked it. And by the time Blaise hit the stage, my hands trembled. Tingled, even. It started up my leg as he began his bullshit spiel about his family and his plans for the people of Florida and his party.

"We could all learn something from the great Americans who traveled west and turned this great state into what it is today!" The applause was thunderous, the crowd eating his bullshit faster than he could shovel it across the stage.

I bit the inside of my jaw to keep from groaning as he brought his pretty, underweight blue blood wife on stage along with his three adorable children. Then his chief of staff and his junior press secretary, smiling and glad-handing them, before he brought Sabrina, his *girlfriend*, on stage.

And that was my cue.

Sabrina walked across the stage in her cotton candy pink Chanel suit, and that's when the twenty foot screen behind them faded from Blaise's good looks and charming smile to the first photo. Blaise with Missy Keane, the family's sixteen-year-old babysitter canoodling in the back seat of his silver Aston Martin. Next was Shannon Bell, the fifteen-year-old chef's apprentice in her chef coat and a denim micro mini, Blaise's hand between her legs and his lips on her throat.

Photo after photo went up of Blaise's different underaged indiscretions but I saved the best part for last. Indigo Prescott's face came up first, her blonde hair cut in damn near the same style as his wife's and her smiling face young and vibrant. Next was the photo of Tricia Patterson, looking way too young and grubby in a halter top and denim cutoffs and beside her the same image on a Missing Person poster.

The gasps from the crowd were deafening and Blaise was still oblivious. It was fucking glorious. The outraged cries grew louder and the disappointed groans from the men were probably because he'd gotten caught. Or worse, gotten caught on camera. I stood with a satisfied smile as several journalists scribbled furiously on notepads and iPads while a few discreetly captured the images playing on a loop on the screen.

I slipped out of the ballroom feeling just a smidge lighter as I dodged gamblers and revelers on my way out of this oxygen-deprived place. My eyes were peeled for trouble, because no doubt Blaise had decided to use his muscle as a precaution. I hadn't spotted them yet, but I could feel eyes on me.

Fucking paranoia was a bitch. "Excuse me, are you Genevieve Montgomery?" The guy could fill up a barn door nicely.

"No." I took a step around him and kept walking.

"I think you are," he said as he walked beside me, reeking of government work.

"I don't give a fuck what you think."

He took two steps forward and stood in front of me and I had no problem going around him. "Agent Ryan, FBI Las Vegas office."

"Congratulations." The guy was a bit on edge for a Fed and immediately I was on alert, sliding my hand into my clutch purse.

"I'd like to talk to you for a minute."

"Nothing to say and if you have something to say, you should do it with my attorney." He shocked me by grabbing my arm and yanking me against him. I screamed my ass off, hoping to draw the attention of any of the people standing around gawking.

"Shut the fuck up!" He pressed his hand over my mouth and nose and I stomped his foot with my nude stiletto. Agent Ryan wasn't fazed, and he dragged me away outside toward his car I was sure, which I knew meant certain death for me. I couldn't be sure if he was working for Blaise or Rizzoli and in the moment, it didn't matter.

And I wouldn't fucking stop trying to get away because the more progress he made, the more certain my death would be. I bit his hand. Hard.

"Asshole!" I said as soon as my mouth was free.

"Bitch!" he answered, smacking me with his left hand so it didn't hurt as much as it could have. Also, it gave me the chance to get away. I pumped my legs hard out on the street shouting, "Agent Ryan, Las Vegas field office. Supervising Agent Robert Stevens! Address 10975 Beacham Drive. Henderson!"

But he cut me off again with his big fucking hand. I sent my head swinging back right into his nose.

"You'll pay for that bitch!"

I didn't realize I'd run right in the direction of his car. Fuck.

He got the door open and shoved me into the front seat in one practiced move and when I slid to the other side in a desperate escape attempt, he was there with a hard fist aimed right at my eye.

This wasn't going to end well.

# Chapter Twenty-Three

*Jag*

"Jag, we have a big fucking problem, man." Lasso's deep voice and southern twang sent a chill down my spine.

"What?" I stood in the doorway of the ballroom where Rocky promised me Vivi would be as she took down Blaise. The good news was that Blaise and his family were hurrying off the stage while his security and the event coordinators ran helter skelter trying to stop the images on the screen. I could tell they didn't even know where they were coming from. That was my girl. But where was she?

"She's not here," Lasso said.

Rocky had promised she would be in the ballroom, which meant I just missed her.

"Max has eyes on Vivi with some brown-haired dude who looks like a cop."

"Max? What the hell is he doing here?"

Lasso grinned. "You didn't think we'd let you come alone, did you?" I had actually, but I was grateful that it wasn't just me and Lasso.

"Shit." Lasso had his phone glued to his ear. "He's got her in a car. Black Nissan, Nevada plates."

My heart stopped but my feet were already moving toward the door. To Vivi. "Shit, we need to move fast. Who knows where he took her? Or why?"

It was the whys that were driving me fucking crazy. If that dude was working for Rizzoli, then he'd hand Vivi over to that asshole and let him act out every sick fantasy he'd ever had.

"Fuck! If I'd just been there with her."

"Jag, man come on. Worry about that shit later. Right now we need to get your girl." Lasso clapped me on the back and we hauled ass to our bikes, Lasso still on the phone with Max who was close behind the car.

My phone rang but I was already speeding up Las Vegas Boulevard, so I tapped the headset in my helmet.

# HEAVENLY HACKED

"Yeah?" It was Vivi's voice and a man's. The man was angry.

"What the fuck do you care about a bunch of bikers? They're scum." His voice was dark and angry.

Vivi laughed. "You're working with Rizzoli who's the scummiest of all of them." He made a strangled noise that pulled another laugh from Vivi. "Yeah Agent Ryan, you're not the only asshole who can dig. No matter what you do to me, you're in deep shit."

He laughed. "You're full of shit, little girl. If you had anything on me, you would've known who I was."

"I did know. I just didn't realize you were crazy enough to kidnap me in public. It's a good thing I found those not-so-secret emails with Rizzoli about trying to start a gang war. *And* those payments for trafficking those poor young girls. And you know who appreciated it most of all? Agent Hewitt."

There was a smack or maybe it was a punch, but if it was a punch I would fucking put him in the ground.

Vivi's grunt hit me right in the gut but my girl, she was too tough to cry.

"Bitch," the Fed muttered under his breath.

"I've been called worse but I'm sure that's what the boys in Cell Block C will call you when they pass you around, filling your tight little asshole with hot sticky come."

I could hear the tremor of fear in her voice, so I knew the asshole Fed could too.

"Keep talking, bitch, and you'll end up just another body in the desert." He sounded serious and I hoped Vivi heeded his warning.

But of course she didn't as she continued to give him shit. "Either way, you're going down. Sure, you got me by showing up here at the casino, but the damage has been done. My guess is that right now your entire field office is searching for you. Probably already tracking this monstrosity."

Damn, she was taunting that unstable asshole. Didn't she realize he wouldn't hesitate to retaliate?

## HEAVENLY HACKED

"You're bluffing," he accused.

"It doesn't matter to me. I have contingency plan upon contingency plan. Do you?"

Vivi let out a grunt as that fucker landed another blow but it slowly morphed into a laugh. "Did you know your wife, Camille, is fucking the professor that lives two doors down from you? Probably you suspected, but did you know that she's been fucking him since before little Adam was born?"

Stitch zoomed past us in the SUV with a wave, speeding so fast that we lost sight of him quickly. I nodded to Lasso and we sped up too, pushing the next half-mile until the Nissan came into view. And like the good fucking soldier he was, Stitch was in place ready to ram them off the road. He straddled both lanes while Vivi had Agent Ryan distracted. Stitch pitted the car, making it spin and kick up dirt until it came to a stop at a weird angle, nose first into the ravine.

Two gun shots sounded, and my heart stopped just as I dropped the kickstand on the bike and rushed to get Vivi. I was either going to rescue her or murder a federal agent. Either way, that motherfucker was dead. My feet moved faster than they had since I was a scrawny assed-kid running away from bullies, pulling her from the car and frantically checking her for injuries.

"Christ, Vivi. Say something." She had a large gash on her forehead and her pulse was racing so I knew she was fine. "Dammit, Vivi!"

"Quit your bellyaching Jeremiah, I've got a massive fucking headache. You ever been hit with a gun?"

"Yeah. Hurts like a motherfucker, don't it?"

"Even worse." She smiled and only winced a little when I cupped her face to make sure she was all right.

"Nice wig. Maybe you can keep it?" It was inappropriate and the wrong timing, but it made her smile brighter and she opened her eyes.

"Blue?"

"I'm undercover."

## HEAVENLY HACKED

I smirked at her words and helped her stand. "You scared the hell out of me." Vivi sagged against me, proof of just how much this whole day had affected her.

"Watch out, Jag!" I turned at the sound of Lasso's voice, and sure enough, Ryan had his sights set on me or Vivi. Maybe both of us. His gun was already pointed at us, finger dancing with the trigger. I didn't have enough time to get to my gun before he shot but Vivi didn't think twice about pulling her blade and aiming it at Agent Ryan.

The knife sliced the air with a wicked zinging sound and landed in his gut.

"Cunt!" he barked, then grinned, lifting the gun again but not before shots rang out. Two of them, hitting him right in the chest, sending that asshole to hell where he belonged.

With a gasp, Vivi turned and a small smile lit her face. "Agent Hewitt, I presume?"

He nodded and walked closer to us. I pulled Vivi closer and slightly behind me. "I am. Nice to meet you

Vivi and I'm sorry it took so long but bureaucracy can be a real bitch."

"Thanks for the assist back there." She began to sag against me even more as shock set in and the adrenaline began to wear off. Realizing her display of vulnerability, she stood straight. Shoulders squared.

"It's me who owes you a thanks. That guy would've gotten me killed and probably a bunch of your friends, too."

She nodded, skin looking paler by the second. When the EMS arrived and rushed to her, Vivi tried to brush them off. "I'm fine. Really."

"Vivi, let him check you out. Please."

She nodded and followed behind the paramedic. "I will but only because I'm feeling a little woozy," she said, her voice breathless.

I followed, not liking how unsteady her legs were and the way her words began to drag. "Wait!" I ordered.

She turned with a smile. "You gonna carry me, Jag?"

# HEAVENLY HACKED

"Damn straight." My feet began to move as a shot rang out and everyone ducked. Everyone but Vivi, who looked at me in shock.

"Jeremiah, I think—" she looked down at her shoulder and the growing red circle and then back to me. "Damn." Then she collapsed right before my eyes.

I couldn't take my eyes off Vivi, even as shots flew out all around us. A crash sounded in the distance and more shots sounded but my concern was her.

"You have to move," the EMS said as he shoved me aside, ripping Vivi's jacket to get to the wound in her left shoulder.

They stopped the flow of blood and got Vivi on a gurney and into the ambulance. I sat beside her in the back, looking at the smoking red pickup truck smashed against a guardrail as we sped past on our way to the hospital.

Good fucking riddance.

## Chapter Twenty-Four

*Vivi*

"Do you know who shot me?" I asked the question at the same time Jag asked one of his own. Sort of.

"I want you to stay, Vivi. Here in Vegas. You and me. Together."

Jag flashed that gorgeous irresistible smile and my heart leapt and twerked with happiness even though I knew it couldn't last.

"Say something," he urged from across the black and white checkered tablecloth of one of our favorite greasy spoon diners near Jag's house.

I didn't know what to say because telling him the truth would break his heart, but I couldn't lie. Not to Jag. "I know, and I want that too."

He frowned and sat back in his chair, his gaze searing a hole right through me. "Why does it sound like there's a 'but' coming?"

My smile was bittersweet. "Because you're a smart man." I didn't want to tell him this, not today. Not ever but I'd put it off for the past three days while I was in the hospital and now, well now I was out of time. "I do want to stay Jag, but I can't."

"Is it because of the guys? If so, I'll talk to them and we can quash this shit, Vivi." Anguish filled his brown eyes and my heart split right down the middle.

"No Jag. I don't give a shit about them, I give a shit about you." I placed my right hand on top of his because my left one was still in a sling thanks to the bullet that went straight through my shoulder. "This is killing me, Jag. I need you to know that and I don't say it lightly."

"I know." And his slight smile told me he did.

"Bob stopped by while I was in the hospital," I admitted.

"Shit. She's still alive?"

"I know, right? But yeah, she's a little battered but fine." Bob was strong and a seasoned CIA agent. Very little left her shaken. "But I'm not."

"What's that mean?" He held my hand between his, thumb stroking the pulse racing on my wrist.

"It means that I can't stay here. Not now and not for a while."

I couldn't believe my eyes were burning with unshed tears, but they were. It was a strange sensation, one that felt so out of place and totally fucking out of character for me that I didn't recognize what it was at first. Tears. I was crying. Over Jag.

"I broke a lot of laws Jag. A lot."

"You did it to stay alive because Slauson dropped the fucking ball!" He was upset, and I didn't blame him. But...

"That doesn't change anything, Jag. You know the shady shit the government can do when they want something." And they wanted me.

"You're not telling me something. Dammit, Vivi. What's going on? Do you not want this?"

"Don't be a crazy fucker. Of course, I do. I came here to find Jeremiah and to see if he was still the nicest boy I'd ever met and could help me. Instead I found you. Jag. Big and strong, but still the nicest person I've ever known. You went against your club, your brothers for me and no one has ever cared that much for me. Ever."

"I'd do it all over again just to keep you safe."

I believed him. "Good because that's exactly why you're not going to make this harder, Jag. You and the Reckless Bastards, you broke a lot of laws, too."

He froze, and I could see the tension fill his body. It was finally sinking in, now that the danger was behind us, just how much shit we'd done in the name of survival.

"Shit. How much trouble are we in?"

"None. Because I'm taking care of it. Eighteen months of indentured servitude to the government and our slates are wiped clean. Unless of course they try to extend the time, which I fully anticipate."

"I can't let you do that, Vivi. I won't take it so don't fucking ask me to."

I stood gingerly, nearly knocking into the waitress as she dropped the food on the table. After three days of hospital food, it all smelled so good but I wasn't about the food right now.

I was pretty sure Jag was about to see a side of me he never thought he'd witness. Sliding in beside him, I turned to face him.

"I'm not asking, Jag. It's done. If I don't do this, we're all getting charged. Let me do this. You have a life here. A family. A full life of people who give a damn about you. I know what that means, and I won't let you give it up."

"Not even for you?" He cupped my face and I blinked, the unfamiliar warmth of tears streaming down my cheeks.

"Especially not for me, Jag." I took a deep breath to slow the pounding in my chest, but it didn't work. "I love you," I blurted out, inelegantly and unceremoniously.

His eyes flashed surprise and his beautiful lush lips pulled into a heart-stopping smile.

"Do you? That's damn good to hear because I would've felt pretty fucking stupid telling you that I love you and I refuse to live without you, if you didn't feel the same way."

In that moment something clicked into place inside of me. A feeling of peace, of coming home. Rightness. Jag was all of those things for me. Everything I'd been avoiding and running from my whole life. It felt like I'd never belonged more in this moment.

"We're a fine fucking mess, aren't we?"

"No babe, we're a beautiful fucking mess. The beautiful-*est*." Jag cupped the back of my neck and slowly lowered his mouth to mine, teasing my lips with his before his tongue joined in, sliding and massaging my own. The kiss grew deeper in stages until it was all consuming. Jag ate at my mouth, devouring me like he just couldn't help it. Like it was me, the orphan with mad computer skills, who was driving him to the point of insanity. He pulled back, smiling and out of breath.

"I'm not letting you go Vivi. Not ever."

"Good, because as soon as I'm finished with the government, I'm comin' for you Jag. You can count on that, babe."

I kissed him, again. Harder this time because I knew Bob was waiting for me and I had to go. "While I'm gone, take care of those Roadkill fucktards because when I get back I'm going to need a lot of alone time with you. A lot."

His grin came slow and seductive, his hand still cupping the back of my neck as he pressed our foreheads together.

"I love you, Jag."

"I love you too, Vivi."

"I'll be back as soon as I can."

"I can't fucking wait, babe."

I slid out of the booth and stood. "I'm not going to say goodbye." I turned toward the door and walked without looking back. I'd never met Jeremiah before now and I knew God, or my angels, or the universe were watching over us back then.

And I hoped like hell they were watching over us now.

Walking away from him was the hardest thing I'd ever have to do.

\* \* \* \*

## ~ THE END ~

## Acknowledgements

Thank you so much for making my books a success! I appreciate all of you! Thanks to all of my beta readers, street teamers, ARC readers and Facebook fans. Y'all are THE BEST!

And a huge very special thanks to Jessie! I'm such a *hot mess, but without your keen sense of organization and skills, I'd be a burny fiery inferno of hot mess!! Thank you!

And a very special thanks to my editors (who sometimes have to work all through the night! *See HOT MESS above!) Thank you for making my words make sense.

Copyright © 2018 KB Winters and BookBoyfriends Publishing LLC

# KB WINTERS

## About The Author

KB Winters is a Wall Street Journal and USA Today Bestselling Author of steamy hot books about Bikers, Billionaires, Bad Boys and Badass Military Men. Just the way you like them. She has an addiction to caffeine, tattoos and hard-bodied alpha males. The men in her books are very sexy, protective and sometimes bossy, her ladies are…well…*bossier*!

Living in sunny Southern California, with her five kids and three fur babies, this embarrassingly hopeless romantic writes every chance she gets!

You can reach me at Facebook.com/kbwintersauthor and at kbwintersauthor@gmail.com

Copyright © 2018 KB Winters and BookBoyfriends Publishing LLC

Printed in Great Britain
by Amazon